She Could Feel Steve Standing Behind Her

She jumped in surprise when his hand came to rest on her hair just below her shoulders.

"Don't tell me I frightened you again," he said, chuckling. "You did know I was here."

"I . . . Well, I . . ."

"Your hair is so beautiful. It felt wonderful under my fingertips when we were dancing. Did I thank you for wearing it down for me?"

"I . . ." God, he was turning her into a mumble mouth again!

"My mother raised me to always say thank-you," Steve said, slowly turning Jade around by the shoulders to face him.

Oh, help! This wasn't going right at all! He was definitely about to kiss her and they hadn't even had coffee yet! His eyes were turning that smoky gray that meant . . .

Dear Reader,

Welcome to Silhouette! Our goal is to give you hours of unbeatable reading pleasure, and we hope you'll enjoy each month's six new Silhouette Desires. These sensual, provocative love stories are both believable and compelling—sometimes they're poignant, sometimes humorous, but always enjoyable.

Indulge yourself. Experience all the passion and excitement of falling in love along with our heroine as she meets the irresistible man of her dreams and together they overcome all obstacles in the path to a happy ending.

If this is your first Desire, I hope it'll be the first of many. If you're already a Silhouette Desire reader, thanks for your support! Look for some of your favorite authors in the coming months: Stephanie James, Diana Palmer, Dixie Browning, Ann Major and Doreen Owens Malek, to name just a few.

Happy reading!

Isabel Swift
Senior Editor

SDRL-7/85

ROBIN ELLIOTT
Picture of Love

Silhouette Desire

Published by Silhouette Books New York

America's Publisher of Contemporary Romance

SILHOUETTE BOOKS
300 E. 42nd St., New York, N.Y. 10017

Copyright © 1986 by Joan Elliott Pickart

ISBN: 0-373-05261-8

First Silhouette Books printing February 1986

America's Publisher of Contemporary Romance

Printed in the U.S.A.

Books by Robin Elliott

Silhouette Desire

Call It Love #213
To Have It All #237
Picture of Love #261

ROBIN ELLIOTT

lives in Arizona with her husband and three daughters. Formerly employed in a high-school library, she is now devoting her time to writing romance novels. She also writes under her own name, Joan Elliott Pickart.

For Oleta North,
a writer's friend extraordinaire. Thanks, Oleta.
Keep spreading that sunshine.

One

Darn it," Jade said, planting her hands on her slim hips and looking down the narrow road. "Where is that rotten kid?"

Two heavy blond pigtails flapped against Jade's full breasts as she turned and stomped to the backyard of the cabin, where she surveyed the pile of tar paper and shingles before turning her brown eyes upward to scan the storm clouds. If that Haskins boy didn't show up to repair the roof before the rain started, she'd wring his neck! Ben McKenna had assured Jade that the Haskins clan was a reliable bunch, so where was Billy Haskins?

"Don't you dare!" Jade said, as a distant rumble of thunder danced a cadence through the sky.

Jade returned to the front of the cabin and started down the dirt road. Her long slender legs carried her quickly forward as she jammed her hands into the pockets of her cutoffs, a scowl on her pretty face. If the

Haskins brat was strolling along taking his own sweet time getting there, she'd yank him up by the collar and haul him to the cabin. Where was his sense of responsibility, for Pete's sake?

Large trees cast shadows over the path, and the leaves rustled in the increasing wind preceding the coming storm. One drop, just one drop of rain on her hardwood floors and she'd strangle that...

Suddenly Jade stopped in her tracks as a movement in the grass along the edge of the road caught her eye. It was probably a squirrel or rabbit or... Good Lord! It was a foot! A large, paint-stained-tennis-shoe-clad foot! Oh God, there was a dead body on her property! No, the foot had moved, so it wasn't a corpse.

Jade moved forward cautiously, leaning over slightly as she approached the foot. It was connected to a tanned ankle that was connected to a muscular calf that was connected to... Good grief, she sounded like that silly song. She had to get a grip on herself! The man—The Foot was obviously male—could be dying, for all she knew, and might need her help.

Jade pushed aside a low bush and stepped into a grassy clearing under a large tree. The Foot became a Body! Jade's eyes flicked over the massive form that was clad in paint-spattered khaki shorts and a faded yellow T-shirt. He was huge, had to be six-foot-four, and a broad chest moved steadily up and down. A nicely muscled, tanned arm lay spread out on the grass, while his other hand rested on his stomach.

Jade bent over and peered at the face. A crop of curly black hair covered his head. Dark eyebrows slanted above closed eyes that boasted a thick fringe of lashes. A straight nose, high cheekbones and soft full lips completed the face. The body was absolutely gor-

geous! Never in her twenty-six years had Jade seen a
man that oozed such blatant sexuality, and he wasn't
even moving!

The body moaned slightly and Jade jumped in startled surprise. Was this Billy Haskins? Had he suffered
some kind of injury on the way to her cabin? No, that
didn't make sense. Ben had spoken of the Haskins boys,
and this was a man. Lord, was he ever! He had to be in
his late thirties, but Ben was pushing seventy so maybe
to him this was a mere pup.

Now what? The only way to find out if he was hurt
would be to try to wake him. Sound reasoning. But
what if he came up swinging? She'd be dead meat. If he
decked her, she'd be out cold for a week!

Jade reached up to a maple tree and pulled off a twig
that had a leaf at one end. She dropped to her knees
about two feet from The Body's chest. She slowly lowered the twig until the leaf brushed against the straight
tanned nose.

Nothing.

She put a little more wrist action into her efforts and
the man she thought of as "The Body" lifted his hand
from his stomach and attempted to shove away the
nuisance. Encouraged, Jade wiggled her weapon with
vigor. He still hadn't opened his eyes, but surely...

"Oh God!" she screamed, as The Body suddenly
lunged into the air, grabbed her by the upper arms and
threw her backward onto the ground, the massive form
pinning her in place.

She stared wide-eyed into eyes that were either blue
or gray, she wasn't sure which, and she swallowed
heavily before attempting to speak. "Hello," she said
weakly.

"What in the ... ?" The Body said, shaking his head as if to clear the cobwebs.

His voice was deep, appropriate for a man of his size, and those eyes really were the most remarkable color. But this was hardly the moment to be assessing his charms, she reminded herself. "Would you get off of me?" she said, hoping she sounded really indignant.

"I'm not carrying a wallet, if that's what you were after."

"What?"

"You should have gone for the watch."

"Huh?"

"You can always fence a good watch."

"I wasn't trying to rob you! I thought you were dead! Then when you weren't, I was trying to find out if you were hurt. Do I look like a pickpocket? Now, get your carcass off of me or I'll scream!"

"Go ahead. There's no one around for miles." He smiled, flashing straight white teeth against the tanned face.

He was so beautiful it was enough to make a person weep. Too bad he was ... what? A rapist? Oh Lord! He had to be Billy Haskins. He just had to be. He'd simply stopped to take a little snooze. "Are you planning on fixing my roof?" Jade asked hopefully.

"Your what?"

"You're Billy Haskins, right? On the way to repair Jade Sinclair's cabin? Well, guess what? I'm Jade, and if you hurry along you can get it done before it starts to rain. Good idea? Yes! Excellent. So just haul yourself up and off we'll go."

"Your roof." The Body nodded thoughtfully. "Before it rains."

"Very good!"

"There's something I have to do first."

"Oh?"

"If I'm going to remove myself from you, I should do the polite thing and kiss you goodbye."

"Not necessary. I—"

Jade stopped speaking and watched in detached fascination as The Body slowly, slowly lowered his head toward her. A tingling sensation of anticipation swept through her as his lips came closer and closer. They brushed over hers in a fleeting motion, then returned in the next instant to take full possession of her mouth.

The kiss was incredible. It was the softest, sweetest kiss Jade had ever experienced. A flickering tongue sought entry to the dark regions of her mouth, and Jade complied before she realized what she had done. Her eyes drifted shut as she relished the taste, the feel, of his lips moving against hers.

Her hands seemed to possess a will of their own as they crept up to the strong back hovering above her, where she felt rock-hard muscles bunch under her fingertips. His lips were intensifying their claim on hers, and a tingling heat started in the pit of Jade's stomach and began to work its way throughout her. She felt dreamy, as if she were floating, as tongues met and drew lazy circles around one another. It was wonderful. It was ecstasy. It was all so...terrible! This shouldn't be happening!

"Stop that!" Jade gasped, wrenching her head away.

"Let's call that one 'hello,'" The Body said, his voice slightly strained, "and now let's do 'goodbye.'"

"No!"

"Why not, Jade Sinclair?"

Yeah, why not? It was so nice! "Because... umm...you have to fix my roof."

"Before it rains."

"Yes."

"Well," he said with a sigh, "if duty calls, then I guess we'll say goodbye later."

With agonizing slowness, The Body pushed himself up. Jade immediately felt chilled without the heat that had emanated from him. He stood erect and extended his large hand to Jade, drew her to her feet and then carefully straightened her braids. Jade took a sharp breath as his knuckles moved over the fullness of her breasts that pushed against the thin material of her plaid cotton blouse. She stepped back and looked up at him, her eyes locking onto the unusual coloring of his in a long studying gaze that seemed to go on and on.

"Your roof?" he finally said quietly, breaking the strange spell that had drifted over them.

"My what? Oh! Of course!" Jade said, walking back out to the road. "I must say, Billy, if you contract to do a job, you shouldn't stop for a nap."

"I thoroughly agree," he said, falling in step beside her.

"Ben McKenna said you were very reliable and that you do very good work."

"My *work* has never gotten any complaints," he said, a small ironic smile tugging at the corners of his mouth.

"I bet," Jade muttered, resisting the urge to press her fingertips to her lips that still pulsated from the passionate kiss.

A deep throaty chuckle caused her to look up in surprise and she received a wide grin from Billy Haskins. He didn't look like a Billy; they were cute. This man was masculinity personified. Jade redirected her gaze to the dirt road, but not before catching a glimpse of corded thighs pushing against the paint-stained shorts. He looked more like a football player than a handyman.

"What happened to your roof?" he asked pleasantly.

"It has holes in it."

"I gathered that. From a storm?"

"Neglect, I'm afraid," Jade said, sighing. "I haven't been able to get up here in quite a while, and I was just sick when I saw it. Granny would be so upset."

"Granny?"

"My grandmother. The cabin was her home until she died six months ago."

"I'm sorry. Grandmothers are special people," he said, in a voice so sincere that Jade believed he really did feel badly about Granny.

"Yes, she was," she said softly.

"So you're fixing it up for a summer home?"

"Or longer. I haven't decided."

"You're thinking of living here in Dunrovin?"

"Maybe." Jade nodded.

"Are you?"

"Am I what?"

"Done roving, ready to settle down in a quiet spot like this. You're awfully young for such a secluded place."

"And you're rather old not to show up for a job on time," Jade shot back.

"Being thirty-eight doesn't guarantee a person an automatic sense of responsibility."

"Obviously."

"Looks nice," he said, as they approached the cabin. "Cozy."

"The supplies are around back."

They walked to the rear of the cabin, and he immediately climbed the ladder leaning against the building to inspect the problem.

"Not too bad," he said, jumping off about halfway down. "There's only three or four spots that need repairing."

"I'll let you get started. That storm is really rolling in. I don't want rain on my hardwood floors."

"Got it. I'll be done in a flash."

"Doesn't anyone refer to you as Bill or William?"

"No, I've never been called either. Why?"

"You just don't look like a Billy."

"I don't?"

"Not really."

"Your name suits you, though. Jade is smooth and lovely to touch. It feels good in your hands. It's rather mysterious, too, because it's sort of cloudy like it's protecting precious secrets. You definitely live up to your title, Jade Sinclair."

"Oh," she said quietly, and turned and walked into the cabin through the back door.

Oh? That was the most intelligent thing she could say? The man had just about caressed her with his words, stroked her in a velvet softness with the rich timbre of his voice, and she said, Oh?

"Lord," Jade said, leaning against the door after she closed it behind her. What was there about him? First she had returned his kiss like a sex-starved whatever, and then she was transformed into a mumble mouth when he made idle comments about her name. Idle? Ha! He knew exactly what he was doing. A little verbal seduction there, folks. Billy Haskins was a slick operator. Darn it, he just *didn't look* like a Billy!

Jade jumped as a pounding noise started directly over her head, and she glared at the ceiling before moving to the sink to wash her hands. From the gleaming refrigerator she pulled a package of meat and a variety of vegetables to make stew, then stopped for a moment to nod in approval at the cheerful room.

Jade had soothed a fussing Granny two years before and insisted on having the kitchen completely remodeled with gleaming yellow appliances—including a dishwasher Granny had refused to use. Butcher-block countertops matched the table and chairs, and the no-wax tile on the floor resembled cobblestones. Perky yellow-and-white checked curtains hung at the window over the stainless-steel sink, where Jade was now scrubbing the vegetables with a wire brush.

Granny had really sputtered when Jade had declared she was to have central heating and air-conditioning, but the project had been completed. So had the job of restoring the hardwood floors to a gleaming finish. Granny would have the best, Jade had decided, and had hugged away the old woman's frowns. Granny, however, had sat on the edge of the claw-foot tub in the bathroom and refused to budge when the plumbers arrived. No one was touching *her* tub, by golly, and the room was modernized around her, leaving the bathtub in place.

Jade smiled as she worked, recalling the sparkle in her grandmother's eyes when Jade had brought the wallpaper sample books to make selections for the two bedrooms. That was more like it, Granny had said, and she'd spent hours scrutinizing the books. The cabin had been transformed into a picture-perfect home, and Jade rested more comfortably in her apartment in Detroit knowing that Granny was as snug as a bug in the pretty woods of northern Michigan.

Dear, wonderful Granny, who had been the steadying loving force in Jade's life. Granny had always been there, ready to receive Jade into her warm embrace and kiss away the pain and disappointments that life brought. The cabin would be filled with the aroma of freshly baked bread or cinnamon rolls, and Granny would be in her favorite rocker by the hearth, a smile on her soft wrinkled face, a lavender-scented hankie in her apron pocket. She would set aside the ever-present needlepoint and lift her arms to gather Jade to her breast.

And now Granny was gone. It still seemed impossible to Jade, and she brushed a tear off her cheek with the back of her hand as she vigorously scraped the carrots. Jade missed Granny so very much, she still could not stop the flow of tears that always lay near the surface whenever she thought of her grandmother.

"Oh!" Jade gasped, startled out of her reverie by the ladder being set against the cabin directly in front of the window.

A head of curly dark hair moved past in a blur, followed by the muscled chest, and then he stopped, leaving Jade staring at his paint-stained shorts, corded thighs and the rest of his tanned legs. Jade blinked her eyes once slowly and gave herself a firm mental directive to return to her veggies, but she didn't move. She just stood there, her eyes glued to the scene before her. She was aware of the fine layer of black hair on the legs, of the narrow hips, the flat plane of the stomach that inched above the waistband of the shorts. It was as though he had been chiseled from stone, then smoothed and bronzed to perfection. No flaws in the workmanship, no slip of the sculptor's hand had marred the beauty of the work, and Jade felt her heart start to beat erratically. A warm glow started deep within her, finally showing itself as a heated flush on her cheeks.

She was gawking at the man's torso like some kind of Peeping Tom, for Pete's sake. How disgusting! But damn, she had never seen such raw virility, such powerful masculinity all wrapped up in one economy-size package. The man was incredible!

Suddenly the head connected to the body leaned over and flashed a dazzling smile at her. "Enjoying the view?" he said, loud enough for Jade to hear through the window. "It'll cost you a buck."

Jade spun around and marched to the stove, where she flung the cubes of meat into the frying pan with resounding thuds. She knew she was blushing. Twenty-six years old and she was blushing! What an arrogant creep to assume she had been looking at his...his person. Of course, she had been doing exactly that but...that was beside the point! He was just too cocky! Handymen were supposed to be docile creatures who said, "Yes, ma'am," and went quietly about their assigned chores.

This guy, Jade had to admit, shaking her head, was getting to her. He was setting off sparks within her that were unsettling to say the least. She knew plenty of men who were just as good-looking, had equally nice physiques and... Who was she kidding? This one was definitely a cut above the rest. And he knew it, the louse! Ol' Billy had just better hurry it up on that roof and then haul it out of there!

For the next hour, Jade completed the preparation for the stew and set it on the stove to simmer, then made a batch of corn bread. The pounding above her head continued and was accompanied by a steady roll of thunder. Then, with one tremendous crash from the sky, the heavens opened and began to dump a heavy load of rain. The sound of hammering went on for several more minutes, then the man jumped from the ladder and covered the remaining supplies with a tarp, which he carefully secured against the rising wind. Jade watched from the window, seeing the torrent of rain beating against him as he completed his task. He turned and dashed for the cabin and in the next instant was a dripping mountain in her kitchen.

"Whew!" he said, rubbing his hands briskly over his arms. "It dropped twenty degrees real fast out there. Got the roof done just in time."

"You're wet," Jade said, looking at the growing puddle on the floor.

"True, and cold. Have you got a towel?"

"Oh, yes, of course," Jade said. She hurried into the bathroom and returned with a fluffy pink one.

Jade stared as the man rubbed the towel vigorously over his hair and down his face and arms. He tugged off his sodden shoes and then stood there peering at himself. "This won't work," he said. "I'm soaked. I'll have to take my clothes off."

"I beg your pardon?"

"Can I borrow a blanket to wrap up in?"

"I really don't think—"

"I'm catching pneumonia! Do you want my death on your hands?"

"I thought you were 'dead' when I met you," Jade said, turning on her heel and heading into the bedroom for a blanket. "Here," she said, shoving it inside his hands.

Jade frowned as the man left the room. Wonderful. She really needed this. A naked man wrapped in a blanket wandering around her cabin. She turned the burner on under the coffeepot and went into the living room to set a match to the logs and kindling already laid in the fireplace. The flames immediately leaped up, sending a warm glow over the room.

"Gangway," the man said. "I need heat!"

Jade backed quickly out of his path and watched as he leaned over and rubbed his hands together in front of the fire. The blanket was tucked in at his waist, and her nose was inches away from a smooth tanned back that bunched with muscles as he continued to work the circulation in his hands. Jade swallowed thickly before even attempting to speak, praying she would sound slightly bored.

"Where are your clothes?" It had squeaked. Her damn voice had squeaked!

"In the bathtub."

"Dumb. Bring them out here and put them on the hearth to dry. I'm going to go mop up the mess you made in the kitchen," she said haughtily, striding from the room.

Jade carefully dried the floor with rags and then went into the laundry room to hang them over the washtub to dry. Coming back into the kitchen, her eyes widened as she saw the man bringing a spoonful of her stew to his mouth.

"Needs salt," he said over his shoulder.

"Do you mind?" Jade said, walking over to him and snatching the spoon out of his hand, allowing herself just the teeniest glimpse of the mass of curly black hair on his chest.

"It does!" he said. "It really needs salt."

"Thank you, Julia Child," she said, slamming the lid back on the pot.

"Want me to set the table? I don't expect you to act like a maid when we have dinner."

"What!"

"Where's the stuff?" he said, pulling a drawer open.

"Who said anything about your eating here?"

"The stew is ready, even if it does need salt, the coffee is perked, it's that time of day and I can't leave in this storm. Makes perfect sense to me." He shrugged. "Your phone is ringing."

"I know that!" Jade said, hurrying to snatch the receiver off the hook.

Jade listened to the voice on the other end, managed to say, "I already took care of it, thanks. I appreciate your calling," and hung up. On trembling legs, she moved back to the stove and picked up a long-handled cooking fork, which she held out in front of her with a shaking hand.

"Don't you move!" she said, causing the man to turn around in surprise from the drawer he was searching through.

"What is your problem?"

"That . . . that was Billy Haskins on the phone, saying his truck broke down and he just made it back in to call me. You are a phony!"

"Phony? Me?" The man grinned, leaning back against the counter and crossing his arms loosely over his bare chest. "Are you going to stick me with that thing?"

"If you come near me I will!"

"You and what army?" He chuckled.

"Don't pull a macho shot on me, buster. I want you out of this house!"

"Give me that," he said, reaching out a long arm and taking the fork out of Jade's hand, "before you hurt yourself."

"Who are you?" Jade said, backing up several steps. "The Michigan Murderer?"

"The who? Never heard of him."

"I bet there is one!"

"Probably, but I'm not it."

"Why did you say you were Billy Haskins?" Jade said, her voice quivering.

"I didn't, you did."

"I did no such thing. Or did I?" she asked, shaking her head slightly. "And why were you crawling around on my roof?"

"You told me to fix it before it started raining, remember?"

"That's when I thought you were... Who in the hell are you?" she shrieked.

"Steve."

"Steve?"

"Steve Chastain."

"I knew it! I just knew you didn't look like a Billy!"

"Want me to tell you again how perfectly the name Jade suits *you*?"

"No!"

"Can we eat now? I'm starving."

"Are you crazy? That's it, isn't it? You're a lunatic escaped from somewhere. Oh God, I'm a dead person," Jade said, her hands flying to her cheeks.

"You have an overactive imagination, Jade Sinclair," Steve said with a laugh. "You're going to give yourself nightmares. I'm perfectly harmless."

"Ha!"

"Relatively speaking, of course."

"Meaning?"

"I have fond memories of that lovely kiss we shared on the grass under the tree. If you'll recall, that was 'hello.' We still haven't taken care of 'goodbye.'"

"Oh God," Jade whispered, sinking onto a chair by the table as her legs refused to hold her up for another moment.

"It *was* a nice kiss, Jade," he said softly, "and you enjoyed it as much as I did."

He was right about that much, Jade thought. God, was she bonkers? She had to get him out of there! "Look, it was a funny joke," she said, "but it's over. I'd appreciate it if you'd just leave."

"In this weather? Don't be silly. It's really roaring out there. I don't know what you're worried about. I told you who I am."

"Big deal! Is the fact that you're Steve Chastain supposed to make me feel better?"

"Sure. I'm a nice guy."

"Who says?"

"My parents. They're crazy about me, think I'm top-notch. Call up and ask them."

"I can't believe this," Jade said with a moan.

"You're getting upset," Steve said soothingly. "What you need is a good meal to settle you down. I'll serve up this stew and we'll dig in. What's this? Corn bread? Great, I love it."

Jade watched in detached horror as Steve Chastain proceeded to assemble the dinner and bring it to the table in several trips. She was limp, absolutely could not move a muscle in her body, as he sat down opposite her and smiled. Who and what was Steve Chastain? she thought wildly. Why couldn't he be nice little Billy Haskins?

"You're not eating, Jade."

"What? Oh, yes I am," she said, shoveling a spoonful of stew into her mouth. Oh God, what if he really
was a dangerous lunatic?

"Jade?"

"Don't strangle me!" she shrieked, dropping her
spoon.

"For heaven's sake, woman," he said with a frown.
"Would you stop that? I'm not going to hurt you! Ask
me anything you want—within reason, of course."

"How will I know if you're telling the truth?"

"Watch my nose and see if it grows."

"I'm slipping over the edge," Jade said, rolling her
eyes to the thundering heavens.

"Okay, listen up," Steve said firmly. "You see before you one Steven Robert Chastain, who lives across
the lake on a part-time basis. I rowed over in my nice
little boat, took a stroll and decided to stretch out under a tree. The next thing I know, this pickpocket—"

"I am no such thing!"

"Sorry. This lovely pigtailed person is making strange
advances on my body and—"

"I did not!"

"*And*, after kissing the hell out of me, she orders me
up a ladder to fix her roof! Now, I ask you, was that
socially acceptable behavior on her part? No! But being
the good old boy that I am, I comply with her wishes
only to have my character insulted. Michigan Murderer, indeed! That was not nice, Jade Sinclair."

"Well, excuse me," she said, smacking her palm on
the table. "Ow!"

"You sure are crabby, Jade," Steve said, spreading
butter on a large square of corn bread.

"You really live across the lake?"

"Yep."

"And you just happened to fall asleep under my tree?"

"Yep."

"And you're a sane, law-abiding citizen?"

"Yep."

"Thank God," Jade said, collapsing in her chair. "I'm going to live to see twenty-seven."

"Yep, unless the Michigan Murderer drops by."

"Cute. Pass the salt, please."

"I told you it needed—"

"Don't push it, Chastain. Oh, I owe you some money for fixing my roof."

"That's okay. I'm having dinner, and then there's breakfast tomorrow morning and—"

"Hold it! You're leaving here as soon as your clothes are dry."

"Not I, sweet Jade. I know these June storms. It's socked in good. I don't have a penchant for suicide, so I'm not about to row across that lake tonight."

"Walk around!"

"I'll catch my death. Face it, I'm staying."

"Over my dead body!"

"I'd love to be over your body, Jade, but I'd prefer it very much alive. And warm, smooth, wanting me to make beautiful love to—"

"Would you stop!"

"Do you have a hang-up about sex?"

"Of course not!"

"Good."

"What I mean is . . . Oh, forget it!"

"You're getting hyper again, Jade. You really should relax and eat. You're a very good cook except for the salt problem."

"You're too kind." Jade frowned and reached for a piece of corn bread.

"So, Jade Sinclair, tell me about yourself."

"No."

"Why not?"

"Granny taught me not to speak to strange men."

"I'm not strange, I'm perfectly normal. Besides, we know each other very well. That was you kissing me under the tree, wasn't it?"

"Tree? What tree?"

"Oh, forget it. Pass the salt," he said with a growl.

Jade plunked the shaker in front of his bowl, and they consumed the rest of the meal in silence.

"Thank you," Steve said finally. "It really was excellent."

"And I thank you for repairing my roof."

"I'll help you clean up."

"No, I—"

"You've got a dishwasher. It won't take us long."

Jade knew it was a bad idea when Steve suggested it. He seemed to fill up the room! Every time she turned around he was there, and twice she bumped into his chest, which turned out to be a rock-hard wall.

When the pots were all scrubbed and the table and counters clean, Jade flicked on the dishwasher and began pushing in the chairs at the table, lining them up directly across from one another.

"You're really a neat-freak, aren't you?" Steve said.

"I like things tidy, in order."

"Including your life?" he asked, following her into the living room.

"Yes, I suppose so."

"Interesting."

Steve built up the fire and then sat down on the sofa, stretching his long legs out in front of him and crossing them at the ankles. He looked ridiculous sitting there in the fuzzy blue blanket, and a bubble of laughter escaped Jade's lips as she rocked in Granny's chair by the hearth.

"Is something amusing?" he asked.

"You're not exactly a fashion plate," Jade said with a smile.

"This?" he said, looking at the blanket. "Shall I take it off?"

"No!"

"Just thought I'd ask. So, where do you live when you're not hiding out in Dunrovin?"

"I'm not hiding."

"Figure of speech."

"I live in Detroit."

"Ah, the big city, with its bright lights and glitter. What do you do?"

"I own Grandmother's Cottage."

"I assumed that, since you're in it."

"No, it's my company. I have three boutiques—in Detroit, Westland and Midland. We specialize in hand-crafted needlepoint kits. No two canvases are alike. Each of the shops is decorated like a cozy cottage, and the customers often stay there to work on their projects."

"Are you successful?"

"Very."

"Rich?"

"Very."

"Good for you, Jade Sinclair." He nodded, stretching his arms out across the top of the sofa.

The gesture caused the blanket to slip lower on his hips, and Jade felt the rush of warmth creeping up on her again. It was too much, it really was! The man simply had to put some clothes on! She reached over and pressed her hand on top of his shirt lying on the hearth, only to find to her dismay that it was still damp.

"Am I bothering you?" Steve asked quietly. "You know, sitting around practically nude?"

"Of course not. So," she said, immediately aware that her voice was too loud, "what do you do for money to pay the bills?"

"I'm a promoter."

"Of what?"

"People. I manage the subsidiary contracts of movie stars, baseball and football players, that type. I arrange television commercials, T-shirts, posters, faces on cereal boxes, the whole bit."

"Sounds interesting."

"Most of the time. Some of my clients get a bit wearing on the nerves because of the size of their egos."

"Are you successful?" Jade asked.

"Very."

"Rich?"

"Very."

"Good for you, Steve Chastain," Jade said, bursting into laughter.

"That's a nice sound, Jade. You should do that more often. You've very beautiful when you're smiling. The rest of the time you seem awfully tense."

"This has not been a run-of-the-mill day."

"I'm sorry if I frightened you."

"It will be a funny story in five or ten years." She smiled. "Where's your home, Steve?"

"I travel a great deal. I have apartments in Detroit, Houston, L.A. I built the house across the lake with the idea of having a real home to come to. I guess I was really referring to myself when I spoke of hiding out here."

Jade studied Steve as she heard the weariness in his voice, saw the frown creasing his brow as he stared into the fire. He suddenly seemed miles away, as if lost in his own thoughts, and she kept silent, respecting his quiet moment. The wind howled outside the cabin, and the rain beat against the windows as if seeking entry to the cozy haven within.

"I'm sorry," Steve said, breaking the silence. "I guess I wandered off."

"I've been known to do that. Maybe it's a sign of genius."

"Oh, at least," he said, smiling. "How do you wear your hair when it's not in braids?"

"Pardon me?"

"I bet it's lovely when it's tumbling down your back and floating around your face. I can imagine it spread out over a pillow where I could sink my hands into it. You are a beautiful, beautiful woman, Jade."

Jade could not breathe! Steve was doing it again. He was caressing her, stroking her with words spoken in a low husky voice as his eyes locked onto hers and held her immobile. A crackling tension seemed to fill the air as Jade finally tore her gaze from his and looked into the flames, her heart racing.

"I want to make love to you, Jade Sinclair," Steve said softly.

Two

―――

"For heaven's sake," Jade snapped angrily, "why don't you just come right out with it, Steve? I mean, don't beat around the bush or anything."

"Honesty is the best policy," he said with a smile. "I was simply stating the truth. I do want to—"

"I heard you!"

"And?"

"And forget it! What do you think I am?"

"A very desirable, very lovely woman."

"That's it!" she said, getting to her feet.

"Why are you angry? I certainly wouldn't be offended if you said you found *me* attractive."

"I don't!"

"No? Oh. That was your twin sister I kissed, and who kissed me back, under the tree?"

"Would you quit bringing up that damn tree!"

"Okay. I'll erase it from my mind and concentrate only on the kiss."

"Sweet heaven!" Jade said, stomping into the kitchen. "You're driving me crazy."

Jade poured herself a glass of milk and drank it while she leaned against the counter. Steven Robert Chastain was insufferable. And rude. High-handed and conceited. He was in *her* home, wearing *her* blanket, after eating *her* food, and he had the gall to...to what? He hadn't even touched her. This was the United States of America, with freedom of speech, and all he had done was talk. Granted, it was pretty sexy after-dinner conversation, but maybe she'd overreacted. Steve didn't know that her senses kept whirling out of control from the closeness of his half-naked body. It wasn't his fault she was acting like a ninny. She had just finished telling him she was a highly successful businesswoman, and then she turned around and behaved like a virginal schoolgirl. Not exactly a class-act performance.

Jade washed and dried the glass and placed it back in the cupboard before plastering a smile on her face and returning to her rocking chair. Steve had not moved and sat looking into the fire.

"How long will you be in Dunrovin?" she asked pleasantly.

"I'm not sure. I've placed some of my accounts in the hands of my junior executives and a lot depends on the reactions of the clients."

"You mean they'll deal only with you?"

"I hope not. I really need some time off. I have intelligent competent people working for me who can certainly handle the responsibility. What about you? Can you afford to be up here if you have three boutiques to run?"

"There isn't much for me to do. I have managers in each, a centralized bookkeeping system, everything. I just wander around trying to look important."

"That's the neat-freak in you. You've organized yourself out of a job, so to speak."

"That's the story of my life."

"Meaning?"

"I always do that, Steve. I whip in, assess the situation, straighten out the problems and end up...bored out of my mind."

"It's a gift to be able to—"

"It's a pain. I don't rest until I have it running like clockwork, and then I have nothing to do. I programmed myself into graduating from Wayne State University in three years instead of four. Then I became interested in needlepoint because Granny had always made her own designs, and whamo! Here I am, owner of three stores, have more money than I know what to do with and I'm sitting around sucking my thumb."

"So now what?"

"I don't know. I'm thinking about compiling a group of old letters that belonged to Granny's mother. They're all in a trunk and need to be sorted and deciphered. I thought it would be a nice memorial to Granny."

"I'm sure she'd be very pleased. Won't someone in Detroit miss you if you stay up here any length of time?"

"A man, for instance?"

"You're very astute. Yes, I'm trying to find out if you're involved with anyone, Jade."

"No, not at the moment."

"I'm very glad to hear that." He smiled.

"I'm not about to ask why," Jade said, frowning.

Why had she done that? she thought. She had sat there and told Steve Chastain her innermost thoughts as easily as if she were chatting about the weather. Only her closest friends knew Jade's compulsion to attain her goals and her emptiness when the task was completed. Why had she given a total stranger such privileged private information about herself, the part of her she considered a definite flaw?

Jade had been so positive that the Grandmother's Cottage endeavor would be the answer, that this time she would find a long-lasting challenge. But here she was, restless and empty again, having overachieved herself right out of being needed. She was, vulnerable, lonely and depressed and, damn it, now Steve Chastain knew it!

"Check my clothes and see if they're dry, will you?" Steve asked. "This blanket is getting itchy."

"They're nice and toasty," Jade said, after placing her hand on the warm material.

"Good," he said, pushing himself to his feet. "I'll get dressed. In the bathroom, of course."

"Of course."

Jade rocked slowly back and forth, leaning her head against the high wooden back of the chair. God, she was tired. Emotionally drained. Yet she knew she wouldn't sleep that night. She was tense, a bundle of nerves after rushing from Detroit yesterday in a state of near panic. She had felt closed in, trapped within an existence that once again offered her nothing. Steve had asked if there was a special man in her life. Hardly. There was no time to devote to a serious relationship while she was hellbent on one of her missions, so of course there was no one waiting in the wings when it was completed. Oh, she dated constantly, attended the flashiest parties, went to the grand opening of everything that opened, but the men were just friends or acquaintances, eager to escort a pretty woman for the evening.

And she *was* pretty. She knew it, and could use it to her advantage when the situation arose. Like everything else, it had come easy. Learn the tricks of hairstyles, simple yet effective makeup, the proper clothes to accentuate her nice figure, and then just put it all in motion. Nothing to it.

But that summed up her life. Nothing to it. If only Granny were there to help her, to listen and soothe away the inner pain. Granny always knew just what to say to help Jade pick up the pieces and start over with a determined tilt to her chin. But Granny was gone and Jade was completely, absolutely alone.

"Jade?"

"What!" she shrieked, jumping to her feet. "Oh, Steve, you scared me!"

"You're sure edgy." He smiled. "Is the storm bothering you?"

"No, not at all," she said. "Would you care for a brandy?"

"Yes, that sounds perfect."

"How're the clothes?" Jade asked as she moved to pour the drinks, averting her eyes from the T-shirt that stretched tightly across Steve's chest.

"A little stiff, but warm," he said, sitting back down on the sofa.

Jade frowned as she saw that her hands were trembling slightly when she handed Steve his snifter. She had just gotten used to him sitting around half-naked, and now she was getting rattled because he was dressed! But the way the T-shirt and shorts molded themselves to that perfectly proportioned body wasn't even playing fair!

"Have you ever been married, Jade?" Steve asked, as she sat back down in the rocker.

"How do you know that I'm not?"

"You said you weren't involved with anyone. Answer the question."

"No, I have never been married. Have you?"

"I am."

"You are!" Jade said. God, had she yelled that? she thought wildly. Someone please tell her she hadn't yelled!

"To my work," he said, amusement showing in his whatever-color-they-were eyes.

"Common ailment among the mega-bucks boys of this world," Jade said. "What color are your eyes?"

"Where did that come from?"

"They're driving me nuts. First I think they're blue, then I decide they're gray."

"They're neither—or both."

"Confusing."

"That's the breaks." He shrugged.

"If you wear a blue shirt, do they look blue?"

"Well, yeah."

"And if you wear gray?"

"Yes, but this is rather embarrassing."

"Why? You did a lengthy number on my hair."

Steve put his head back and roared with merriment, the sound rich, seeming to rumble up from his chest, and Jade smiled. A man's laughter was echoing through Granny's cabin, an event that had never happened before. God, it sounded good.

"Okay," Steve said, shaking his head, "score one for you. You're quite a woman, Jade Sinclair."

"Do I say thank you?"

"Indeed you do. It was a sincere compliment."

"Then, thank you."

"Will you have dinner with me tomorrow night? We could drive into Midland."

"I . . . yes, that sounds lovely."

"I'll pick you up at seven. That's providing it stops raining so I can go home in the meantime."

"You'd better," she said laughing, "or my reputation will be shot. Gossip travels fast around these woods."

"Did you grow up here?"

"When my mother wasn't shuffling me around, yes. Granny raised me right here in this cabin. My mother would swoop in every once in a while and drag me off, but for the most part Dunrovin was my home."

"Where's your mother now?"

"Living in the south of France with husband number five. This one is younger than I am, I think. I really don't remember what she said."

"She doesn't sound terrific. Are you bitter about it, Jade?"

"Heavens no! I had Granny. You're coming across like a shrink, Steve. Goodness."

"I'm just trying to get to know you better, understand what makes you tick. It's important."

"Why?"

"Because then I can avoid saying or doing anything to hurt you. I would never want to make you unhappy, Jade."

"You don't even know me."

"Yes, I do," he said, swirling the amber liquid in his glass.

Yes, I do. Three dumb little words spoken in a voice so soft it seemed to fall over Jade like a benevolent cloak. Oh, how lovely it would be to have someone who really knew and understood her, but that seemed impossible.

"Jade, where do you go when you get that faraway look in your eyes?" Steve asked quietly.

"Disneyland."

"Do you have a nice time?" He chuckled.

"Sure. Everyone has fun at Disneyland. I think the rain is letting up."

"Are you trying to get rid of me?"

"No, I'm resigned to the fact that you're spending the night. On that sofa."

"I'm too tall for this thing."

"This isn't the Holiday Inn, bub."

"There are two doors in the hall. Tell me there's another bedroom."

"There is, but no bed."

"Wonderful."

"There used to be a bed, but it kind of sagged so we tossed it out the door. I was going to get another one but just never got around to it. When I came to visit Granny I just camped out on the sofa. Being five-foot-six—a normal-size person, you understand—I fit just fine."

"All right already! So I'll hang over the end and never walk properly again. It doesn't matter. It really doesn't."

"That's good," Jade said happily.

"Oh, Jade," Steve laughed softly, shaking his head, "you're like a breath of fresh air. I never know what to expect from you. Frightened one minute, funny the next. But I can't help wondering if you're happy."

"Is anyone totally content?"

"I imagine. If they don't set unachievable goals for themselves. They get where they want to go and then sit back and enjoy it."

"And you, Steve?"

"Me? I'm satisfied with my life about eighty percent of the time. Then it all piles up, like now, and I'm ready to chuck it. But I won't. I'll relax for a while and then go right back to the rat race."

"This rat would love a race to run in. I'm fresh out." Jade frowned.

"Let's trade. I'll do needlepoint and you deal with egotistical superstars."

"Grim. I'll pass. Are you finished with your brandy? I'll take your glass."

"Thanks," he said, handing her the snifter.

Jade immediately got up and walked into the kitchen, flicked on the light and busied herself washing and drying the glasses. When she turned around she bumped into Steve's chest.

"Why did you do that?" he asked.

"I didn't know you were there."

"I don't mean walk into me. I mean, why did you jump up and wash the glasses?"

"Because they were dirty."

"Haven't you ever left a mess somewhere? You know, toothpaste in the sink, underwear on the floor?"

"No."

"Never?"

"Never," Jade said, acutely aware that Steve had not moved and was leaning slightly toward her, causing her to back up against the counter.

"You need to loosen up, Jade."

"I do?" she said weakly.

"Oh, yes. You're a bundle of nerves, like a coiled spring. You'll get an ulcer or something."

"I have a cast-iron stomach." Steve was going to kiss her and she knew it, and for the life of her Jade could not come up with one firm objection to the plan.

"You know I'm going to kiss you, don't you?" he said softly.

"I sort of figured that out."

"I just thought I'd warn you."

"That's very considerate of you, Steve." God, what an asinine thing to say! But then she'd been acting rather weird around this man ever since she found him "dead" by the road. So he was going to kiss her. How big a deal could it be?

The kiss was like the Fourth of July fireworks display on the Detroit River! Steve cupped her face in his large hands and claimed her mouth in a sweet gentle embrace that tasted like brandy. Almost immediately it intensified as his questing tongue sought and found hers, sending a delicious shiver down Jade's spine.

Her arms moved to circle Steve's neck, her fingertips inching into the thick curls as she urged him closer, relishing the sensations that swept through her body. Steve's hands went from her face to her back, pressing her breasts against his hard chest as his mouth continued to ravish hers in a series of feverish passionate kisses. And then those strong hands inched lower, over the sloping roundness of Jade's buttocks as he pulled her into the contours of his body, Jade feeling his arousal, his bold announcement of need for what she could give him.

It was heaven. All the turmoil and confusion was swept from Jade's mind and replaced by infinite bliss. The strength and energy in Steve's rugged length that Jade had been reacting to for all those hours was now directed at her, consuming her, stroking, caressing and wanting her. And she wanted him! For now, for this moment in time, she would step away from herself and become nothing more than a woman who would go to her man, to give and receive, and rejoice in the splendor of their union.

A soft moan escaped Jade as Steve's hands slid up to find her full breasts. His thumb flicked across the taut nipples that throbbed through the thin material of her bra and blouse. His touch was torture and ecstasy combined, making Jade ache for more, needing Steve to quell the fire of passion that ran rampant within her.

Suddenly Steve stepped back and drew a ragged breath. Jade looked up at him in a dreamlike state of confusion, seeing his eyes that seemed a deep smoky gray and emanated readable desire.

"As I said, Jade," he said, his voice strangely thick, "you're a very beautiful, very desirable woman."

"Steve, I—"

"That was not the goodbye kiss I owed you from under the tree."

"It wasn't?" she asked, her voice a hushed whisper.

"We're going to forget about saying goodbye. We'll concentrate on a lot of hellos."

"How lovely," she purred, hoping he couldn't hear the thunderous beating of her heart. "I...think I'll bid you good night now. It's been a long day."

"All right," he said, moving completely away from her. Jade saw him wipe a fine film of perspiration from his brow with this thumb.

Ah-ha, Jade thought, walking into the living room. Stoic Steve was just as shook up by that hot-and-heavy-in-the-kitchen number as she was. So why had he stopped? Didn't he want her? Of course he did! Every inch of that gorgeous body had been ready, willing and able! And she had practically torn the clothes off that luscious . . .

Jade had to stop her thoughts from the dangerous turn they were taking. She turned to Steve, who was following her. "Where's your blanket?"

"In the bathtub."

"Good grief!" she said, going to retrieve it, then pulling a pillow off the closet shelf. "Here," she said, dumping them on the sofa.

"Jade, I wanted you," Steve said quietly.

"Well, I—"

"And you wanted me. But it's too soon, too fast. We're doing this right, Jade. There's more to us than just going to bed together. Understand?"

"Not really."

"You will. Good night."

"Night," she said, turning and walking into her bedroom and shutting the door.

She pulled off her clothes, placed them carefully in the hamper, and set her tennis shoes neatly under the dresser. As tired as she was, she undid the thick braids and tugged a brush through her tangled tresses. After washing her face, she folded up the bedspread and set it on a chair, slipped into a long bright red flannel nightie and crawled into bed.

Jade punched her pillow and flopped over onto her stomach, only to immediately turn again and stare up into the darkness. What had Steve meant by that pretty little speech? What "more" was there going to be between them? And just what was it that they were going to do so all-fired "right?" He had a lot of nerve deciding it was too soon, too fast, as he had so eloquently put it, to go falling into bed together. Since when had Steve Chastain been elected spokesman for their group of two? Of course, he was absolutely right, and she would have been mortified in the morning, but still, he sure was pushy!

She'd better think this through. She had responded to Steve's kiss with an abandon she wouldn't have thought herself capable of. He had been slowly stoking her fire from the moment she'd found him "dead" by the road. Every movement, gesture, throaty laugh, had sent sparks racing through her, and when he had finally moved in for the kill, she'd melted like so much ice cream. Rotten man! Well, no, not exactly. He was the one who had called a halt to the whole escapade.

Did Steve Chastain make sense? Nope. Had her behavior in the kitchen been even remotely close to reasonable? Nope. Now, here was a good question: Was she sorry it had happened? Definitely, nope. Oh, the hell with it. She couldn't figure it out if she lay there and stewed about it all night. Granny always said things looked better in the morning. Lord! Bring on the morning!

Despite Jade's belief that she was too tense to sleep, she drifted immediately into a peaceful dreamless slumber.

When she opened her eyes again, she stretched leisurely and yawned. The memories of the previous night came instantly to the front of her mind, and she slid off the bed and walked to the bedroom door. She quietly pulled it open, stepped into the hall and peered around the corner. The sofa was empty, the blanket and pillow shoved to one end. Only then did Jade realize that the cabin was flooded with sunlight and she could hear the birds chirping. Apparently Steve had headed back across the lake when he awoke and found that the weather would allow him to make the trip safely.

So be it.

Jade turned to the bedroom and made up the bed, then showered and shampooed her hair while standing under the old-fashioned shower head in the claw-foot tub. After scouring the tub and wiping it clean, she blow-dried her hair and braided it into a single plait down her back.

As she pulled on jeans and a cotton blouse, she thought for a moment she smelled coffee perking, but decided it was only her imagination. She certainly was hungry. Dressed, Jade headed for the kitchen.

"Oh my God," she yelled, clutching her hands to her breasts.

"Did I scare you again?" Steve smiled, then redirected his attention to the stove.

"I thought you were gone."

"Before breakfast? I'd be too weak to row. Sit down. It's almost ready."

Jade sank onto a chair, her eyes widening in horror as she surveyed the kitchen. It was a disaster! It had been vandalized! Eggshells lay strewn over the countertop, where a puddle of a gooey liquid dripped with a maddening steadiness over the edge onto the floor. The cupboards and drawers stood open and various containers were strewn helter-skelter on the table. There was a mound of coffee grounds near the sink, as if Steve had missed during several attempts to spoon it into the pot. It was simply awful! Gross! It would be like eating in a pigsty. The man was an absolute slob!

"Sleep well?" Steve asked pleasantly.

"Very. You?"

"Not exactly. I told you I wouldn't fit on that sofa. I survived, though. Oops."

"Oops?" Jade said, looking at him anxiously.

"Just splashed a little bacon grease on the stove. Nothing serious."

"Oh," Jade said, more in the form of a moan.

"Here we go," Steve said, bringing a platter of scrambled eggs and bacon to the table, then turning to pull a plate full of toast off the counter. "Damn," he said, as the top piece flipped off and landed on the floor.

A close-to-hysteria giggle escaped from Jade's mouth as Steve picked up the toast and tossed it into the sink, leaving a blob of butter stuck to the floor. The health department was going to shut her down. They'd come swooping in the back door at any minute, take one look around and hang a Condemned sign on the wall.

"Silverware," Steve said, rummaging noisily through a drawer. Jade cringed. "There," he said, plunking down the utensils by her plate. "I'll get the coffee."

Jade cautiously filled her plate from the platter, and peered at the offering suspiciously before venturing a small bite. It tasted all right, looked reasonably safe, and the coffee set before her smelled . . . like coffee.

"How is it?" Steve asked.

"Delicious. Do you cook often?"

"I usually don't have time. I enjoy it, though. Sometimes I really make some elaborate meals."

God help his kitchen, Jade thought, reaching for a piece of toast.

"Please excuse my appearance," Steve said, running his hand over his beard-roughened face. "I didn't know I was going to a slumber party so I wasn't prepared."

"That's okay." Jade smiled. "It's not every day I eat breakfast with someone who looks like a borderline bum."

"View it as ruggedly appealing."

"Ugh."

"*You're* very pretty in the morning, Jade. Of course, you're lovely at night, too. I just thought I'd tell you."

"Thanks."

"I wish you had worn your hair loose, though."

"It gets in my way."

"When we go out tonight, will you wear it tumbling down your back?"

"Are you starting your sexy talk again?" she said, turning a frown on him.

"My what?"

"That routine of yours where your voice gets all low and rumbly and you say stuff about gorgeous hair and loveliness and all."

"Do I do that?"

"Yes, and you know it! You must hang out with some gullible women if they fall for that number."

"It doesn't get to you, huh?"

"Don't be ridiculous. Of course not." Was he believing this? Jade thought. She'd sell him some swampland. Did it get to her? It melted her right down to her socks!

"Oh, well," he said with a shrug, "that's okay. I'll just knock you over with my charm."

"You're sick."

"You're cute."

"Brother," she said, rolling her eyes.

"Well, I'll whip this kitchen into shape and—"

"No! I mean, that wouldn't be fair. You cooked, I'll clean."

"But—"

"I insist!"

"If you're sure."

"Oh yes. Yes!"

"Then I'll head on home to clean up."

Jade stood up at the same time Steve did. They remained at opposite ends of the table in a long quiet moment as their eyes met and held.

"I'm not going to kiss you," he said finally. "I might scratch you with my beard."

What was a little blood? She'd heal. "I'll...see you tonight then."

"Yes, ma'am," he said, walking to the door.

"Have a nice day, Steve."

"You too. And Jade? I'm really looking forward to this evening."

Jade stood at the kitchen window and watched until Steve had strode across the clearing on his long legs and disappeared among the trees. Then she spun around and started tossing eggshells into the trash can. An hour later, the kitchen was spotless, the cabin dusted from top to bottom and the blanket and pillow Steve had used were returned to their proper places. Now what? She could start pulling out the old letters, but she really wasn't in the mood. Go for a walk? Write to some friends?

Her eyes lingered on the sofa where Steve had sat—then slept—the previous night, and she recalled the sound of his laughter dancing through the room. The cabin had seemed rather small as he moved through it with his great height and broad shoulders, but now it was strangely empty.

She was, Jade decided, going to have to be on her guard around Steven Robert Chastain. He had happened into her life at a time when her resistance was at a low ebb, and because she had foolishly bared her soul in front of him, he knew it. He might view her as an easy mark to liven up his vacation, and her conduct so far didn't dispute it. Well, tonight would be different. She'd adopt her sophisticated big-city aloofness and show Mr. Chastain that his first impression of her had been incorrect. They would share a nice meal, she'd bid him good night at the door and that would be that.

Very good. Then why did she find that scenario so depressing? What did she want—Steve to throw her down on the braided rug in front of the fire and make mad passionate love to her? Don't be ridiculous. She wasn't even going to kiss him again, let alone... Well, maybe a kiss. Or two. Three max. Damn it, what was it about him? She didn't even like his type, with his cocky self-assured arrogance. But then he'd smile that smile, or give her one of those long mesmerizing gazes, and her pulse would be off and running. The man had sex appeal, no doubt about it.

But it was more than that. Steve Chastain had a depth, a quality about him that Jade had not encountered in her escorts in Detroit. When she spoke, Steve listened, really listened. If there was a touch of sadness in her voice, he frowned. And when she smiled, his expression immediately matched hers. He made her feel important, special and more aware of her femininity than she could ever remember being. He was dangerous to her equilibrium, the organized tidy existence in which she functioned. She was bored out of her mind, but at least she was safe from tall curly-haired Romeos who probably tromped over hearts as easily as eggshells.

And that was another thing! Steve was so sloppy! He hadn't even folded up his blanket. And her kitchen—God, don't think about it again. Not only had he wreaked havoc with her senses, he had practically demolished her house! He was a menace! But, oh, how

Granny would have adored Steve Chastain. She'd cackle that funny little laugh of hers and tell him he sure knew how to fill out a pair of jeans. Then she'd order him onto the sofa and find out all about him as she rocked back and forth and worked on her needlepoint. She'd fix him cinnamon tea and bread and butter, and when he left she'd extract a promise from him to visit again real soon.

But when Steve returned to the cabin that night it would be to see Jade, not Granny. Jade Sinclair would open the door and welcome him, and past that point she did not have the foggiest notion what she was going to do.

"Go for a walk, Jade," she said aloud. "You're driving yourself nuts."

Jade tramped through the woods, drinking in the aroma of the still-moist earth and watching the small animals scurrying through the underbrush. She strolled along the edge of the lake and waved to the fishermen who sat patiently in their boats waiting for the elusive prize to nibble at their hooks. Back at the cabin she ate lunch, cleaned up the kitchen, then called the managers of the Grandmother's Cottage boutiques. All was well, they assured her, business was brisk, and Jade should enjoy her vacation and not give them a second thought.

Frowning, Jade wandered into the second bedroom and opened the trunk. She lifted out the top batch of letters, which were secured by a faded pink ribbon. The paper was yellowed with age and Jade handled it carefully, placing each sheet on the floor as she sat Indian style in front of them. The handwriting was tiny and cramped and she wondered if she would even be able to decipher the correspondence.

Jade leaned over and peered at the papers. This didn't make sense. If someone saved their mail, wouldn't it be from different people in a variety of handwriting? Well, maybe not if it was from a special beau. But wait a minute! Each of the letters started with "Dearest Charles" and was signed "Your loving Emma." Emma was Granny's mother, and she had been married to Henry! Who in the heck was Charles? And what had he done? Saved Emma's letters and given them back to her? Unless . . . she never mailed them!

"Mercy me," Jade said. "What were you up to, Emma old dear?" Absently, Jade glanced at her watch. "Heavens, look at the time!" Where the afternoon had gone, Jade didn't know, but it was getting late. She decided to leave the letters on the floor, figuring it was best not to handle the crumbling paper more than was necessary, and dashed to fill the claw-foot tub with warm lilac-scented water. After pinning the braid on top of her head, she stripped off her clothes and sank up to her chin in the fragrant water.

When the water finally became uncomfortably cool, Jade stepped out, wrapped herself in a fluffy towel, and sat down at the dressing table, where she began pulling her hair loose. She brushed it until it shone, the wheat-colored cascade shimmering down her back.

Wear it up? Wear it down? Steve *had* specifically asked her to leave it loose. Oh, why not? She hadn't worn it that way in ages; she might as well please Steve. But who wanted to please Steve, for Pete's sake?

"Why am I having this debate with myself?" Jade said aloud, shaking her head. "Wear the dumb hair down and forget it!"

Time was passing, and Jade had to dress quickly if she wanted to be ready when Steve arrived. She selected a cap-sleeve cocktail dress—nothing very fancy, but it showed off her figure well, she thought. She felt pretty, feminine and so alive it was almost a prickling sensation. Where was all this exuberance coming from? She was only going out to dinner with Steve. With Steve Chastain, who had crept into her thoughts with disturbing regularity during the hours since she had last seen him.

The sound of a car engine reached Jade's ears just before seven, and she moved quickly to answer the door when she heard two sharp raps.

"Hello, Jade," Steve said quietly, as he stepped into the room. "You look lovely. Your hair is even more beautiful than I dreamed possible."

"I'll get my coat," Jade said, hurrying into the bedroom. My God, he had taken her breath away! She actually felt as though the air had been swept out of her lungs, leaving her light-headed. She knew he wasn't going to show up in his grubby shorts and T-shirt, but my heavens, he was devastating! The expensive black suit was cut to perfection and molded itself to the muscled contours of Steve's body. Combined with the dark tie and white silk shirt that accentuated his curly black hair and rugged tanned complexion, he was…awesome. Lord, she sounded like a teenager. Awesome, indeed. But he was!

Jade took a deep breath, picked up a small clutch purse and the coat that matched her dress and returned to the living room, smiling pleasantly.

"Ready?" Steve asked.

"Yes."

The car was a low-slung silver sports model that roared into action at Steve's command, and they were soon leaving the secluded sleepy town of Dunrovin be-

hind and streaking along the highway to Midland. Jade
was aware of the aroma of a musky after-shave and a
slight scent of soap that emanated from Steve's body.
She was also disturbingly conscious of the stirrings
within her, the heated desire that was once more creeping through her simply because Steve was close to her,
jarring her with his maleness, his sexuality and virility.

A sudden wave of apprehension swept over Jade and
only one thought hammered through her mind. She
wanted to turn around and go home!

Three

Somehow Jade managed to take part in the idle chit-chat with Steve during the drive into Midland. She had perfected the knack of detaching herself just enough so that she could answer intelligently but still carry on a totally separate dialogue with herself in her mind.

She needed this time desperately to get a firm grip on herself. Where Steve Chastain was concerned she was turning into a quivering lump of jelly, and that would never do. It was now the hour to leap into action and get...organized! Heaven knows she was good at *that*. All it would take was a logical assessment of the situation and a precise plan of action that would automatically result in the desired goal of regaining and keeping her composure in Steve's presence. Pure and simply. Easy as pie.

So...do it! But how? How could she analyze something she didn't understand? How could she control

emotions that surged through her of their own voli-
tion? She couldn't even explain her irrational reactions
to Steve, let alone fix them! Oh, hell's bells, what a
mess.

"He's the glamour boy of football," Steve was saying.

"He certainly is handsome," Jade said, right on cue.
"Is he conceited?"

"I don't know how he gets his helmet on. To put it
bluntly, he's a pain in the butt. But he brings in a lot of
money for my company, and my secretaries would shoot
me if they didn't get to drool over him when he comes
into the office. It's all in a day's work."

"And the women? The movie stars?"

"Most are easy on the eyes, but are bubble heads."

"You're not very complimentary." Jade laughed.

"It's just my present frame of mind. I'm burned out
right now."

"So you'll set aside the work and simply play."

"More like relax. Do as little as possible."

"Like jumping in the car and driving all the way into
Midland?"

"This is pure pleasure. After all, look at the company I'm in. That dress is sensational. You must be a
very popular young lady in Detroit. I know I'm proud
to be seen with you tonight. You make me feel possessive. I'm afraid I'll resent anyone even looking at you."

"Good heavens," Jade said with a laugh. "I'm not
that terrific."

"Yes, Jade you are. And you're one of the most interesting women I've ever met. I want to hear about all
the different projects you've conquered in your time.
I'm serious! I'd love to see you in action. It's a fantastic dynamic trait."

"I hate it," Jade said with a frown.

"Only because you've lost touch with yourself, no longer know what you want or need. That's where you have to start, Jade, within yourself."

"What do I do? Call myself up on the phone?"

"Something like that." He chuckled. "Here's the restaurant. I hope you're hungry."

"Always."

In the center of the table where Jade and Steve were seated, a lighted candle sat casting flickering shadows over their faces. Jade was sure she saw Steve's eyes change from blue to gray and back again as the light danced across his features. She had seen the admiring glances they had received as they entered, and she decided they did indeed make a striking couple. Steve discussed the selection of wines with the steward, and Jade and Steve ordered their meal from large flocked menus.

"Find any dead bodies on your property today?" Steve asked, after tasting the wine and nodding in approval.

"No, it's one to a customer." Jade smiled. "I hope."

"Such an auspicious first meeting we had."

" 'Ridiculous' is a better word."

"I rather enjoyed it."

"Do not mention that tree, Steve."

"Right. Want to talk about the kiss in the kitchen instead?"

"No!"

"But it was so very—"

"Steven Robert, hush your mouth."

"You sound like my mother."

"And you sound like a kiss-and-tell teenager."

"Then I'll keep my nice memories to myself."

"Good."

"Did you look over your ancestor's letters today?"

"I barely got started, but it's very interesting already," Jade said, her eyes shining. She quickly explained about Emma being married to Henry, and the mysterious messages to the unknown Charles.

"I wonder," Steve said thoughtfully, "if he was a figment of her imagination, a fantasy she created to fill a void in her life. Or maybe he was real and she worshiped him from afar because he was unobtainable for some reason. You haven't read any of them?"

"Not yet. It's going to be difficult because the writing is very tiny and the paper is discolored."

"Keep me posted on this," Steve said. "It's fascinating. Do you suppose I could see them?"

"Do you really want to?" Jade asked in surprise.

"This has piqued my curiosity. Think about it, Jade! Having an insight into the feelings, emotions, reactions of a whole different generation. And not from a textbook written by someone of today, but in that individual's own handwriting from decades ago. It's very exciting!"

"Yes, I guess it is." Jade nodded. "I was trying to sell myself on this project, but your enthusiasm is infectious. I'll probably be up at the crack of down poring over every word. I hope Emma wasn't terribly unhappy."

"May I come over tomorrow and get in on the action?"

"Sure."

"Great. Oh, I met the real Billy Haskins at Ben McKenna's store today."

"Oh?"

"He's about seventeen, has red hair and freckles. I shook his hand and told him he was my best friend.

He'll probably spread the word that the Chastain guy is slightly wacko.''

"You are!"

"No, just very grateful that little Billy's truck broke down. The conversation went a little haywire, though.''

"What do you mean?"

"Well," Steve said, "I was chatting, you know, telling Ben how I fixed your roof just in time so nothing happened to Granny's hardwood floors.''

"And?"

"He said I was lucky to make it back across the lake alive in that storm.''

"Don't tell me," Jade moaned. "Please do not tell me what you said next.''

"Okay, I won't.''

"What did you say?"

"Well, something to the effect that I had spent the night.''

"You didn't!"

"It somehow came out sounding kind of racy, I guess, because Ben winked at me and slapped me on the back. Well, you'd better believe I was going to straighten him right out and tell him I slept on the sofa, but before I could, this weird woman gasped and ran out of the store.''

"Did she have on a hat?"

"Yeah, with a flower bobbing up and down.''

"Mrs. Steinberg, the biggest gossip of Dunrovin. Steven Chastain, do you know what you've done? She'll have it all the way around the lake by tomorrow that you and I are sleeping together.''

"I told Ben what really happened.''

"Big deal. Mrs. Steinberg has more listeners than the six o'clock news. Oh, this is terrible!"

"We didn't do anything."

"You and I know that but ... Lord, you have a big mouth."

"I was only making friendly conversation," he said, an expression of total innocence on his face. "Want me to find this Mrs. Whoever and tell her she's got it all wrong?"

"No! She'd really eat that up! She'd take that as a sign that we're guilty as sin. Whoever said that women talk too much hadn't been introduced to you yet. I can't believe you actually did that!"

"Your dinner," the waiter said.

"Nice timing," Steve said, smiling.

Jade scowled at Steve and then attacked her steak and lobster with a vengeance, totally ignoring him for several minutes as she concentrated on the delicious food.

"I could string up a big banner outside Ben's store saying, 'I did not sleep with Jade Sinclair,'" Steve said finally.

"Oh, good grief," Jade said, bursting into laughter.

"No?"

"No!"

"I'm only trying to be helpful. Right my wrong. Atone for my sin."

"Would you stop it?" Jade said, still dissolving into merriment.

"Do you forgive me?"

"I'll say yes so you won't do anything rash."

"You have a kind heart, Jade."

"How long have you been coming to Dunrovin?"

"Are we changing the subject?"

"We certainly are," Jade said.

"My house was just completed, so this is really my first extended stay. I came up here last summer with a friend to camp and really liked it. I bought the land and managed to have the outside of the house constructed before the winter set in. The inside was finished later and here I am."

"That explains why I've never heard of you."

"But now you have."

"Me and the rest of Dunrovin! You didn't waste any time making yourself known."

"Are we back to that?" Steve said, grinning at her.

"No. I'll get indigestion." She should be furious at Steve for what he had said in Ben's store. Mrs. Steinberg was going to have a field day with this tidbit. But Steve was so endearing, with his wide-eyed innocence and harebrained schemes to set the matter straight. It was awful and funny at the same time. Oh, well, what was done was done, and Jade wasn't going to ruin the evening over it. Old Lady Steinberg was probably jealous of Jade after getting a glimpse of the hunk of man who had supposedly spent the night ravishing Jade's body. It was more than funny, it was hysterical, and the amusement in Jade's eyes finally erupted in delighted laughter.

"There's that lovely sound again," Steve said.

"The more I think about this thing with Mrs. Steinberg, the better it gets. I would love to have seen her face."

"She looked like a fish, sort of popping her mouth open and closed and nothing coming out. I thought she was going to pass out."

"Do you always stir up trouble wherever you go, Steve?"

"*Moi?* Don't be silly. I'm as pure as the driven snow."

"Bull."

"True, but my mother believes it."

"Mothers are supposed to. It goes with the job."

"Would your Granny have been upset over my little blunder?"

"Heavens no! She would have thoroughly enjoyed it. A few years ago she took care of a baby for a couple of weeks while the mother was ill. Granny sauntered into Ben's with that infant on her hip and made remarks about how much the child looked like me. Need I say that Mrs. Steinberg was in the store? Granny had made certain of that before she went into her performance."

"I think I would have liked your Granny, Jade."

"She would have *adored* you!"

"Would you care for dessert?" the waiter asked.

"Just coffee, please," Jade said.

"Make it two," Steve said.

"Two coffees," the man said, moving away.

"There's a guy at a table over there who's been staring at you all night," Steve said. "I'm going to punch him in the nose."

"Go ahead, but I'm not bailing you out of jail."

"You wouldn't?"

"Nope, but I'd call Mrs. Steinberg and tell her you'd found a new place to sleep."

Their mingled laughter swirled around them, and a sense of peacefulness settled over Jade. It was lovely being in the elegant restaurant with Steve, talking, sharing, feeling carefree. It felt good to know he would be there every time she lifted her eyes, with his mass of curly hair and rugged good looks. Jade basked in his attentiveness, let it wash away the restlessness and inner turmoil, and she simply enjoyed.

It had been so long since someone had talked—really talked—and listened to her. Steve appreciated her beauty, but he made it clear he was interested in her entire person, everything that went into making her who she was. He had called her fascinating, but so was he. Steve Chastain was from a fast-paced world of celebrities and big money. He moved in high society, rubbed elbows with the elite and famous, and yet had expressed excitement over unraveling the mysteries surrounding Jade's great-grandmother. High rollers didn't care about things like that! But Steve did. He was an enigma, a mysterious combination of personalities.

"Would you care to dance, Jade?" Steve asked, bringing her out of her reverie. "There's a band playing in the other room."

"Marvelous," she said, carefully folding her napkin into a neat square before rising to join him.

Chandeliers had been dimmed to produce a glow of intimacy over the dance floor, and the band played slow dreamy music. Steve swept Jade into his arms and moved her across the floor with a gracefulness she would not have thought possible for a man of his size. He ran his hand down the silky cascade of her hair before coming to rest on the small of her back. Jade could feel the heat emanating from Steve's hand through the material of her dress and was aware that her breasts were pressed against the rock hardness of his chest.

God, he felt good, smelled good, and would taste good when he kissed her. And, oh yes, he would kiss her when they returned to her cabin. He would reach out those strong arms, pull her into his embrace and seek and find her mouth. The mere thought of those sensuous lips claiming hers brought a surge of desire into Jade's body, and she shivered slightly under the onslaught.

"Chilly?" Steve asked.

"No, I'm fine."

Steve folded her hand within his and brought it to his chest, where she could detect the steady beating of his heart. Jade nestled closer to him, relishing the feel of the steely muscles moving against her. How nice it was of that band to be playing just for them. To Jade, no one else seemed to exist as she and Steve continued to float over the floor as the hours flew by.

"Uh-oh," Steve said finally, "that drumroll means that's it for tonight."

"But I was having such a lovely time! You're an excellent dancer, Steve."

"So are you, *and* you fit perfectly into my arms. I can't remember when I've enjoyed myself as much as I did tonight, Jade."

Jade just smiled, and they made their way out of the room. Steve delivered a very smooth, very polished line, and Jade knew that was exactly what it was. He was charming, had all the social graces, and had perfected his technique of making his companion of the evening feel as if she were the most important woman on earth. Jade knew all that and didn't care. Why not be the recipient of his charm for a few hours? What harm could it do? His flash and dash no doubt usually lured the lady into his bed, but not in Jade's case. She would invite him in for coffee, thank him again for a lovely time, and send him on his way. Like it or lump it. Boy, was Steven Chastain in for a shock!

Driving home, Steve insisted that Jade direct him to the fashionable mall that housed Grandmother's Cottage, and they got out of the car and looked in the window.

"Even from the little I can see, I'm impressed," he said. "You have three of these?"

"Yes, and I've been approached by several other shopping center managers who want me to come into their complexes."

"Will you?"

"No. Enough is enough. If I flood the market with the concept it will lose its freshness."

"You have an excellent head for business."

"Bigger is not always better."

"Very true. I exercise the same theory in my promotion work. I throw out more ideas than I keep. You know, Jade Sinclair, we have a lot in common."

They chatted comfortably during the drive back to Dunrovin. This time Jade directed her entire attention to the conversation. Steve was well versed on a multitude of topics and the banter was lively, quick and fun. They argued noisily about the virtues of various football teams, and when Jade began rattling off statistics like a computer printout, Steve threw up his hands in defeat. The time passed so quickly that Jade looked up in surprise when Steve turned onto the dirt road leading to her cabin. She immediately invited him in for coffee.

"You sit, I'll fetch," Jade said as she switched on a soft light in the living room.

"Sounds good to me," Steve answered as she headed into the kitchen.

Jade set the coffee to perk and was struggling to reach a tray high in the cupboard when a large tanned hand appeared out of nowhere to help her.

"Here you go, shorty," Steve said, handing it to her.

Where had he come from? Jade had left him safely parked on the sofa and here he was looming over her, looking tall and massive, and seeming to fill the room. She had this all worked out, and the plan did not in-

clude Steve Chastain following her around. It also
didn't include having him take off his jacket and tie and
undo the two top buttons of his shirt.

"Thank you," she mumbled, placing cups and sau-
cers on the tray along with sugar, cream and a plate of
cookies.

Jade stared at the coffeepot, willing it to complete the
job quickly. She could feel Steve standing directly behind her, caught the faint lingering aroma of his after-
shave, and jumped in surprise when his hand came to
rest on her hair just below her shoulders.

"Don't tell me I frightened you again," he said,
chuckling. "You did know I was here."

"I . . . well, I . . ."

"Your hair is so beautiful. It felt wonderful under my
fingertips when we were dancing. Did I thank you for
wearing it down for me?"

"I…" God, he was turning her into a mumble mouth
again!

"My mother raised me to always say thank you,"
Steve said, slowly turning Jade around by the shoulders to face him.

Oh, help! This wasn't going right at all! He was definitely about to kiss her and they hadn't even had coffee yet! And there went his eyes! They were turning that
smoky gray, which meant . . .

Any further mental ramblings Jade might have carried on were obliterated by Steve lowering his head and
claiming her mouth in a searing kiss. As his arms went
around Jade, hers reached up to circle his neck and the
kiss intensified into a long powerful embrace where
tongues sought and found one another, and sweet dark
regions were explored.

The noise of the coffee perking seemed to be drowned out by the loud beating of Jade's heart, which echoed in her ears as she offered no resistance to being pressed into the hard countours of Steve's body. He lifted his head a fraction to draw a ragged breath, and then his lips returned to hers, dominating her whirling senses, rendering her incapable of thinking straight.

"I have now," Steve said, his voice sounding husky as he released her, "said thank you. The coffee is ready."

"The what?" Jade asked.

"The coffee."

"Oh! Of course," she said, spinning around, gritting her teeth as she heard a rumbling chuckle come from Steve's chest.

Somehow Jade managed to pour two cups of coffee, and she voiced no objection when Steve picked up the tray and carried it into the living room to the coffee table. She was trembling so badly she would have sloshed it all over the place. What a rat! Steve had snuck up on her like a nefarious shadow and kissed her with a vehemence that had turned her into a dunderhead. She had to regroup and, for God's sake, get organized! He was going to whip some more of his sexy talk on her, and she had to be ready!

"Jade," Steve said, when he was seated on the sofa and she was in the rocker, "I've been thinking."

I just bet you have, she thought smugly. But she was prepared this time. "Oh?" she said pleasantly.

"You said those letters of Emma's were brittle from age."

"Letters?" Jade said, her eyes widening.

"I have some clear plastic folders we use for photo proofs to protect them from fingerprints. I could bring some with me tomorrow and slide the letters into them. We could still read them and wouldn't have to handle them so often.''

"That's an excellent idea." She nodded absently. He was giving her the crazies!

"All right, I'll bring them along. Is ten o'clock convenient?"

"Yes, that's fine. I always get up early."

"Well," Steve said, draining his cup, "I'd better hit the road."

Jade followed Steve to the front door, where he shrugged into his jacket and turned to look at her. "It was a perfect evening, Jade."

"Yes, I enjoyed it, too."

He tilted up her chin with one long finger and brushed a kiss across her lips in a motion as light and delicate as the flutter of a butterfly's wing. "Good night," he said softly.

And then he was gone.

Gone. Gone? What had happened? One minute he was kissing the breath out of her in the kitchen and the next thing she knew he was gone! Where was the good-bye kiss, the see-you-tomorrow kiss, the let's-make-love kiss? Who in the hell was running this show?

Jade picked up the tray and stomped angrily into the kitchen, where she washed and dried the cups and replaced the cookies in the canister. In her bedroom, she hung the dress on a padded hanger and zipped it into a garment bag before proceeding with her usual night-time rituals, at last slipping into bed in her red flannel nightie.

Steve Chastain was not behaving himself. Heavens, she made him sound like a naughty little boy! In actuality the man had not done one single thing wrong except be unpredictable. Jade was so accustomed to controlling every situation, that Steve's independent actions were throwing her out of kilter. Why hadn't he tried to hustle her into bed so she could adamantly refuse? *That's* how it should have gone. But no, he gives her a chaste little kiss and toddles on his way. Did the dope have a kitchen fetish? Was he turned on by gleaming yellow appliances and stainless steel sinks? That kitchen kiss had been potent stuff! So why had he fizzled out at the front door?

"Men," Jade said, punching her pillow, "are beasts."

Jade was up at dawn and bustling around cleaning what was already clean, fluffing throw pillows on the sofa that were fluffy enough. She arranged the cooking spices in the kitchen cupboard in alphabetical order, then swept out and wiped down the fireplace, which resulted in the need for another shower. She had just redressed in clean jeans and a blue cotton T-shirt and again had her hair in a single braid when she heard Steve's car approaching the cabin.

Tight faded jeans, a much-washed chambray shirt and a dazzling smile greeted Jade when she opened the door. The head of curly black hair appeared slightly damp from a recent shower. A whiff of fresh-smelling soap and the familiar after-shave reached Jade as Steve moved into the living room and she managed nothing more than a weak hello.

"I brought these folders," he said, setting a stack on the sofa.

"Thank you. Coffee?"

"No, thanks, I just had some."

"Then come into my parlor, Mr. Chastain," Jade said breezily, heading for the second bedroom.

Steve scooped up the plastic folders and followed Jade, stepping carefully over the yellowed papers that lay in neat rows on the floor.

"There are two more batches," Jade said, reaching into the trunk, "and they're in no better condition."

"Are they dated?"

"Month and day, but no year."

"Okay. What if we place each in a jacket and then start putting them in chronological order?"

"You're on," Jade said. "Pull up a piece of floor and sit yourself down."

Seated with their backs against the wall, the pair worked in silence, concentrating on not damaging the fragile paper. Steve commented that it seemed unusual that each letter was the same length, none of the messages continuing over to the other side of the sheet. The task completed, they began sorting the plastic folders by date.

"Done," Steve said finally. "Now we can get to the good part."

"Food first. I'm starving," Jade said, pushing herself to her feet. "Can I tempt you with some lunch?"

"There's lots of things you could tempt me with, Jade Sinclair," Steve said, following her out of the room.

There they were again, Jade thought, kissin' in the kitchen. Watch her suddenly turn irresistibly sexy and Steve unable to keep his paws off her. They'd been in that little room for two hours and he hadn't laid a hand on her. Honestly, if he made a move on her out there, she'd label him weird and shuffle him off to Buffalo.

He didn't touch her. Steve simply sat down at the table and watched as Jade prepared chicken salad sandwiches and a plate of fresh fruit and cheese. He didn't talk or offer to help, he just sat there making Jade a nervous wreck. He politely said that a can of soda would be fine and no, thanks, he didn't care for any potato chips. He was a perfect luncheon guest, and Jade was so jittery she slammed the soda roughly onto the table, causing a fountain to squirt out the top.

"Damn it," she said, reaching for a wad of paper towels. "Eat your lunch!"

Steve chuckled, but quickly suppressed his smile when Jade threw him a stormy glare and plunked herself on her chair.

"You're right about the letters," he said, ignoring her expression. "They all say 'Dearest Charles,' and are signed 'Your Loving Emma.' The mystery deepens. Who was Emma's darlin' Charles?"

"I hope she didn't write these when she was twelve years old," Jadē said. "That would really take the spice out of it."

"True. Maybe Charles was a St. Bernard."

"Horrors!"

"A nickname for a girlfriend named Charlene?"

"Steve, where is your romantic flair?"

"On hold," he said, winking at her.

"Sorry I asked."

They finished the meal in a relaxed silence. At last Steve said, "That lunch was great. Let's get back to work."

"I'll just clean up in here first."

"Leave it for now, Jade," he said, grabbing her by the hand and pulling her from the room.

"But…" Jade said, looking over her shoulder at the dirty dishes.

"Emma awaits!" Steve roared, and Jade gave up the battle.

Again they sat on the floor, but Steve suggested they try to decipher the cramped handwriting together, so they ended up side by side. Jade could feel Steve's tight thigh pressing against hers. His jeans and shirt fit him like a second skin, and today his eyes were blue because of the color of his shirt. He wore tennis shoes with no socks, and she noticed he had such pretty ankles. Pretty? As in feminine and delicate? Hardly. The epitome of masculinity was more like it, and Jade again felt the tingling begin in her lower body and creep with insistent fingers throughout her. Drat it, Steve was too...male!

"Forgot something," he said.

"You did?"

"This."

Steve pulled her close by the nape of the neck and kissed her. Not too fleeting nor too rough, the kiss was just right, and Jade had the irrational thought that she'd like about six more of those, please.

"What was that for?" she asked rather breathlessly.

"I always kiss beautiful women who fix chicken salad sandwiches. It's kind of a thing with me. Okay, letter number one, here we come!"

Steve squinted his eyes and frowned at the tiny handwriting while Jade gave a firm directive to her heartbeat to return to a normal rate.

"'Dearest Charles,'" Steve read. "'Today is my twenty-first birthday and—'"

"Yippee!" Jade yelled. "Emma is all grown up. Go on! What's next?"

"I really can't make this out." Steve frowned.

"Let me see. '...And it is a bleak celebration without you here.' Poor Emma. Charles couldn't make it to her party."

"Maybe he got caught in rush hour traffic."

"Cute. All right...mm...'I will save this letter un-til I can give it to you in person as you said you would be moving around...' What's this?"

"'A great deal,' I think," Steve said, peering over Jade's shoulder. "Old Chuck is a traveling salesman."

"Stop it!" Jade laughed, jabbing Steve in the ribs with her elbow. "This is serious!"

"Then why are you laughing?"

"Because you're making me. Now stop it!"

"Okay. Carry on."

"She goes on about having cake and homemade ice cream," Jade said, "and she received a new parasol and three lace handkerchiefs. Later they all went for a stroll."

"They, who?"

"I don't know."

"No mention of Henry?"

"Nope," she said. "Maybe she hadn't met him yet. Here she talks about the weather and then says how much she misses Charles and is praying he is well. That's it."

"Well, no great news flashes there," Steve said.

"Perhaps the next one will have—"

"No, wait a minute, Jade. Why don't we read the second letter tomorrow?"

"What?"

"One a day."

"Like a vitamin?"

"Yes, exactly." Steve nodded. "It will be more fun that way. We'll get a fresh installment every morning."

"Why?"

"There's no big rush here. Our schedules are our own. Look at it like this. Emma lived her life one day at a time. I think it would have more meaning to watch her grow and change slowly. Is it a deal, Jade?"

"It's not particularly efficient, I must say. Besides, I'm dying to know who Charles was. But, well, okay."

"And no peeking when I'm not here?"

"Would I do that?"

"Probably." Steve chuckled. "So you have to promise you won't cheat."

"Brother!"

"Promise?"

"Yes, all right. I'm glad I don't do business with you. You're mean and tough, Steve Chastain."

"And sexy?"

"Nope, but two out of three ain't bad, pal." She was such a liar, Jade thought merrily.

"Come on. Let's walk to Ben McKenna's. I'll buy you a root beer."

"For a root beer, I'd follow you anywhere," Jade said, getting to her feet. "Ta-ta, Emma, see you tomorrow."

Had she just made a standing date with Steve to meet every morning to read Emma's next letter? Yes, that's what had happened all right. Was that a bad situation? No, not really. In fact, it sounded rather nice. A cup of coffee and a Steve Chastain. Not a shabby way to start the day. Throw in one of those nifty kisses here and there, and Emma's letters could become a very stimulating project indeed.

"You look pleased with yourself," Steve said.

"Just thinking about root beer."

They strolled leisurely through the woods on the way to Ben's store, and Steve related an amusing story about one of the uppity movie stars he represented. Jade was comfortable and relaxed, laughing often and enjoying the sound of Steve's rich chuckle.

It hardly seemed possible that she had known him for such a short time, and she was suddenly very glad that Steven Robert Chastain had picked her tree under which to play "dead." If she really analyzed the situation, she shouldn't like him at all. He threw her so many curves, she kept striking out before she could even get to first base. He refused to follow the mental game plans she formulated, keeping her desires stirred. And look at this! He actually had her tramping through the woods, leaving behind a dirty kitchen!

No, Steve was definitely not Jade's type. Then why was she here instead of at the cabin loading the dishwasher? Why did the proposed morning rendezvous hold such appeal? Why did the very sight and sound and aroma of the man cause her stomach to do flip-flops and her heart to beat an erratic cadence in her breast? Why indeed? She didn't know, but she'd figure it out...later. She was too happy and carefree at the moment to tackle the dilemma. Next to her was the most handsome, most appealing man she had ever known. He was blatantly sexy, made her laugh out loud and was going to buy her a root beer! No sense in spoiling such a lovely combination with analytical thoughts. She'd get it all squared away in her head, but right now she just wanted to enjoy!

Four

––––––

"Hi, Ben," Jade said when they entered the store. "How are you?"

"Fine, Jade. Hello there, Steve."

"Ben. The big drinkers are here. We need two cold root beers," Steve said.

"Comin' right up. Take a load off your feet and I'll bring 'em to ya."

Jade and Steve sat in rickety rockers that circled an old-fashioned potbellied stove. Ben McKenna owned a general store that looked like something out of frontier days. The shelves were laden with everything imaginable, yet Ben could reach up and find whatever his customers needed. Large glass jars filled with peppermint sticks and brightly colored jawbreakers sat on the counter. The people of Dunrovin flocked to Ben's to purchase their supplies or simply to sit and chat to pass the time. If you needed to buy it, Ben had it. Wanted to tell it, Ben would listen. When Granny died, Ben had put a black ribbon on the front door and closed the store for the day, an event that had never occurred before.

"Two beers with the root added," Ben said, bringing over the sodas.

"Join us, Ben," Steve said.

"I'll sit my old bones a minute," Ben said, sinking onto a rocker. "Are you as snug as a bug in Granny's cabin, Jade?"

"Oh, yes. Steve fixed the roof and everything else is behaving itself."

"Ah, yes, the roof." Ben crackled merrily. "I imagine all of Dunrovin knows about that by now."

"Mrs. Steinberg," Jade said with a laugh.

"Speak of the devil," Ben muttered, "and we get her."

"Oh, no," Jade moaned.

A plump woman in her sixties wearing a faded cotton dress and heavy laced boots stamped into the store. Today's hat boasted a bright pink panache that tilted forward precariously as she bustled along.

"Ben McKenna," she yelled in a nasal voice, "I need some vanilla extract and don't you be giving me a dusty old bottle that's been on your shelves for ages. I want mine fresh and... Well, now, Jade Sinclair and Steve Chastain. I suppose it's a coincidence that you're here together?"

"Of course not, Mrs. Steinberg," Jade said pleasantly. "Steve and I finished some business we were attending to and decided to walk down for a cool drink."

"Lord." Steve chuckled, smothering his laughter by taking a swig from his soda bottle.

"And then you'll return to your, uh, business?" Mrs. Steinberg said haughtily.

"Well, I wanted to," Jade said, sighing, "but Steve said it will be more fun if we wait until tomorrow. Personally, I could have kept going all day, but it takes both of us to get it right so—"

"Jade Sinclair," Mrs. Steinberg shrieked, "your Granny would turn over in her grave!"

"Granny! It was her idea," Jade said, her eyes wide with innocence. "I can remember her specifically telling me that when she was gone and I had the cabin to myself, I should—"

"I'm dying." Steve gasped, his shoulders shaking with surpressed laughter.

"Of course," Jade rattled on, "Granny didn't know that Steve would happen along, but I'm sure she'd approve. He has so many marvelous innovative ideas. Why, just last night he suggested that we—"

"Sweet Lord in heaven," Mrs. Steinberg said, "I feel faint. I'll pray for your soul, Jade, but I swear it's too late. Forget the vanilla, Ben. I must go home and lie down. You stay away from my cabin, Steve Chastain. I won't have you lurking around!"

"I assure you, Mrs. Steinberg," Steve said, "that I never lurk. Slink through the underbrush, maybe, but I do not lurk."

"Decadent," Mrs. Steinberg said, as she hustled out the door. "Absolutely decadent."

Jade, Steve and Ben dissolved in laughter, Ben smacking his knee and saying he wouldn't have missed Jade's performance for the world.

"Now you've really done it," Steve said, shaking his head. "You scarlet woman, you."

"Me? Well, for heaven's sake, I was merely referring to our project of reading Emma's letters. What's all the fuss about?"

"You," Steve said, waggling a long finger at her, "are a troublemaker."

"Worried about your reputation?"

"Not me; you're the one who grew up here."

Jade just shrugged.

"So what's this about letters?" Ben asked, wiping tears of laughter from his eyes.

"That's what Jade and I are really doing," Steve said. "They belong to Granny's mother."

"Goodness, now that's going back a piece," Ben said. "Emma and Henry raised their family about the time my folks homesteaded these woods. Was wild rough country then. Emma had herself a baby a year, but lost a lot of 'em to the hard winters. I can remember my mama speaking of that."

"Ben, do you know anything about a man named Charles in Emma's life?" Jade asked, leaning forward in her chair.

"Nope, can't say as I do. Henry brought Emma here as a bride and settled in on that land you own now, Jade. Do know Emma named her firstborn Charles, but he died before his second birthday."

"She named Henry's baby after another man?" Jade said. "I bet she was still carrying a torch for Charles. Oh boy, this gets better all the time."

"Question is," Steve said, "why didn't she marry Charles in the first place?"

"You see, Ben," Jade said, "all the letters are addressed to him, not Henry."

"Interesting." Ben nodded. "Let me know what you find out."

"Maybe Jade inherited her naughty streak from Emma," Steve said with a laugh, getting to his feet.

"How insulting!" Jade said, trying to appear indignant.

"I tell you, Jade," Ben chortled, "your Granny would have been proud of you today. She'd have loved every minute of that scene with Mrs. Steinberg. Remember the time Granny was caring for that baby?"

"Indeed I do," Jade said. "Well, we're off. See you soon, Ben."

"Hope so. This is more fun than I've had in ages."

Jade and Steve walked slowly back to the cabin, chatting comfortably about nothing in particular.

"Would you like to come over to my place for dinner tonight?" Steve asked, standing next to his car.

"That sounds nice."

"I'll pick you up at six. Wear jeans. It'll be casual."

"Okay."

"See you later," he said, then suddenly pulled her into his arms and kissed her very thoroughly.

Jade stood and watched until the sports car had disappeared in a swirl of dust before she walked slowly into the cabin. Again the cozy home seemed empty without Steve's presence, void of a vitality and warmth that he seemed to add. He brought so much to her existence simply by being. But Jade knew that by filling her days, her nights, her thoughts with Steve Chastain, she was not facing head-on the crisis in her life. She had embarked on this sojourn to find herself, reclaim an elusive inner peace and plan her next step. Now it seemed all her mental energies were focused on Steve and it was wrong. Very wrong. When he left Dunrovin to return to his fast-paced world, Jade would be no closer to know-

ing who or what she was or wanted. What if she became like the cabin—empty without Steve?

She couldn't allow that to happen. She must keep her
relationship with him in proper perspective. It mustn't
grow into something that would guarantee heartbreak
when it ended. She could do it. Jade had never lost her
heart to a man, and she did not intend to now. Steve
would be kept in a designated slot, not allowed to step
over the line that would render Jade dependent on him
for her happiness. She would reassess her situation, find
a new goal and move on... alone, as she had always
done.

Why did it all sound so bleak? Jade thought, as she
cleaned the neglected kitchen. She wished Granny were
there to offer her encouragement and love as she always had in the past. Well, Jade was all grown-up now,
she reminded herself, and could certainly take care of
herself. Maybe she *should* consider opening another
Grandmother's Cottage. God, if she saw another needlepoint kit right now, she'd scream! But she'd think of
something to do with herself and it would not center
around Steven Robert Chastain!

Jeans, a red sweater, loafers and a tumbling mass of
loose golden hair was the ensemble for the evening, and
Steve smiled his approval when he arrived promptly at
six. He drove the sleek automobile carefully along the
bumpy dirt road edging the lake and then weaved his
way through the scattered trees, away from the lake
when they reached the other side. When he stopped and
turned off the ignition, Jade jumped out of the car, her
eyes wide as she stood in front of Steve's house.

"It's beautiful," she said. "It's absolutely fantastic."

"I'm glad you like it." He smiled. "I would have had it torn down if you didn't."

The A-frame structure was nestled among tall trees and boasted enormous windows that made up the entire front portion. Once inside, Jade knew her mouth was open but she couldn't seem to shut it. There had never been a home like this one in Dunrovin. Thick chocolate carpet stretched across the wide room, and the furniture was massive, the tones warm. A stone fireplace took up nearly one entire wall and was banked on either side by floor-to-ceiling bookshelves. Steve explained that there was a small den off the living room, and two bedrooms with adjoining baths upstairs.

"Oh, Steve," Jade said, her eyes shining, "this isn't a little cabin to come to on the weekends. It's a home! How can you bear to leave it and go back to living in an apartment?"

"I'll let you know. This is my first stay here, remember? Come into the kitchen and talk to me while I cook."

The kitchen was just as lovely as the rest of the house, but with Steve preparing dinner as only he could do, she could barely see the room for the mess. Jade clutched her hands tightly in her lap and sat down at the table, determined not to insult her exuberant host by making any reference to the whatever-it-was that was oozing closer to the edge of the table. She accepted the glass of wine he handed her and commented that something certainly smelled delicious.

"Lasagna," Steve said, glancing at her over his shoulder. "One of my specialties. Say, how's this for a promotion idea? I'll get a football player to do needlepoint sitting in Grandmother's Cottage."

"It's already been done."

"Oh, that's right. How about a rock star? Comedian? Aging actress?"

"No." Jade laughed. "Spare me. Don't think about business, Steve. You're supposed to be on vacation."

"A German shepherd? I have one of those as a client."

"No!"

"Lasagna!"

"Doing needlepoint?"

"No," he said with a laugh, "it's ready to eat. Follow me."

Steve had set a special table in the den, complete with a lace tablecloth and lighted candles. He placed the steaming dish in the center and held Jade's chair for her.

"How lovely. I thought you said it would be casual." She smiled at him as he took the chair opposite her.

"We'll pretend we're all dolled up."

It was fun. The lasagna was hot, spicy and gooey, the wine mellow, the garlic bread crispy. They talked and laughed, recounted the scene with Mrs. Steinberg in Ben's store, and simply had a marvelous time.

"I can't eat another bite," Jade said finally. "It was superb, sir."

"Thank you, ma'am."

"I will now help with the dishes to work off some of what I shoveled in."

"That is forbidden."

"Why?"

"Because," Steve said, "I don't feel like cleaning up right now."

"It will take a chisel to get this off later."

"And later I'll worry about it." He shrugged. "Come into the living room and I'll light a nice fire."

"We could at least soak the worst pans."

"No, Miss Sinclair."

"Load the dishwasher?"

"Jade!"

"I'm moving," she said, marching into the other room.

Steve lit the fire and it crackled, sending warmth into the room's large expanse. They sat on the plush carpet on the floor, their backs against the oatmeal-colored sofa. Steve stretched his long legs out in front of him, crossing them at the ankle, and Jade was immediately aware of how the material of the black cords he wore pulled against his muscular thighs. The open-necked yellow shirt accentuated his deep tan and dark hair, and Jade marveled once again at the effect Steve had on her when he was doing nothing more than just sitting there! Everything about him seemed magnified, his size, aroma, masculinity, and Jade shifted slightly as desire swirled through her body.

She'd never make it. She could not possibly see Steve day after day and not succumb to the passions that plagued her, stalked her with a miscreant force. Just the slightest flicker of imagination brought into crystal clarity the magnificence of his beautifully proportioned body, its strength and power. A further luxury of thought saw him moving above her in all his splendor, quelling her fiery need and taking her beyond reality and reason.

She had never responded to a man the way she did to Steve Chastain, and she was no closer to understanding why that was true. Simply by walking into the room, he was capable of sweeping aside every firm resolve she made when alone. And now here she was in his home, surrounded by the things he had chosen to give it his special touch, and she liked being there. She felt closer to Steve, as if she had been given a further glimpse of who he was. There seemed to be so many facets to his personality and she suddenly wanted to know them all. Even the little things—his favorite color, his taste in music, the books he read—were all part of him and Jade felt a need to share even the trivial.

"Are you at Disneyland again?" Steve asked.

"I'm sorry. I really was off somewhere, wasn't I?"

"It's the fire. I did the same thing the other night at your cabin. There's just something about it," Steve said quietly, "that makes you sort of stop and take a deep breath. I think we all need to do that more often; we live in such a fast-paced world. It's awfully easy to lose track of ourselves, including our values, goals, what we really want. Trouble is, Jade, every time I gaze into a fire and then look inside myself, I don't like what I find."

"But you seem to have everything," Jade said, glancing up at him in surprise.

"Far from it. Oh, I've got money, social status. But I'll tell you something, Jade. I'm . . . lonely as hell. I'm constantly surrounded by people, many of them jump at my command, and yet there's really no one to talk to. I have communicated more with you in a few short days than I have with associates I've known for years. It's good, Jade, what you and I have. I cherish it. I really do."

"You make me feel very special," she said softly. "I guess we met when we were both very much in need of a friend."

"But friendship won't be enough, you know. I want you, Jade. I can't pretend I don't. When I'm close to you, I'm constantly struggling with myself to keep from pulling you into my arms. I'm running out of will-power, beautiful Jade. We're going to have to be very up-front with each other here, because I think about making love to you and I ache inside. If it's not what you want in our relationship, then I'm going to have to back off and put some distance between us. I've never had a conversation like this before in my life. It's just extremely important to me that I don't hurt you.''

And so it had come. The moment of truth. Jade waited for the turmoil to start raging in her mind. The pros and cons, the rights and wrongs, the dos and don'ts, but they never came. She gazed into the smoky gray, desire-filled eyes of Steven Robert Chastain and...knew. Oh yes, they would make love and it would be glorious! They had shared so much, come so far so quickly, and it was time to go further. They would reach out to each other and bring to their union an honesty that was rare and beautiful. A sense of serenity seemed to settle over Jade, and a soft lovely smile came to her lips. Her fingertips reached to rest lightly on Steve's tanned cheek, and he gripped them with a trembling hand.

"I do want you, Steve," she said, her voice a hushed whisper. "I have never desired anyone the way I do you."

"Oh, Jade," Steve moaned, pulling her into his arms. "Jade."

Steve kissed her so gently, so lightly, placing fluttering motions over Jade's eyes, cheeks and down the slender column of her throat. Then he cupped her face in his large hands and gazed into the chocolate-brown depths of her eyes, his own smoky gray ones radiating his message of desire. Steve lowered his head to claim Jade's mouth, his tongue sliding across her lips, seeking and gaining entry to the inner sweetness. Their tongues met as Jade wrapped her arms around Steve's neck, urging him closer.

As their mouths continued to move against one another, his hands slid to the hem of her sweater. He inched it upward, and Jade leaned back to allow it to be drawn up over her head and dropped onto the sofa. Her bra followed, and Steve's eyes roamed over the fullness of her breasts.

"Beautiful," he said, his voice hushed. "You are so beautiful."

Jade unbuttoned Steve's shirt and pulled it free, pushing it away from his broad shoulders. He shrugged out of the material, and Jade ran her hands up his chest and through the curly mass of black hair. Steve took a sharp breath as her palms rested on the male nipples. In a swift motion he turned and lifted Jade slightly off the floor, then lay her in front of the fire as he stretched out beside her. The firelight danced across their naked torsos, one rock hard and tanned, the other soft and ivory.

With almost maddening restraint, Steve placed small kisses across the tops of Jade's breasts until she was aching in anticipation. She gasped with pleasure when he at last drew one rosy bud into his mouth, drawing it to a taut throbbing response. She immediately missed the warmth of his embrace as he moved to the other breast, it too receiving the loving attention. The heated desire in Jade's body swirled into a raging fire. God, how she wanted this man, this Steve Chastain. Never before had she known such burning desire, such a heightened awareness of her femininity, never been so conscious of the marvelous intricate differences between the bodies of man and woman.

Steve undid Jade's jeans and drew them down and away from her slender legs. Next her bikini panties, and she lay before him in naked splendor. Pushing himself to his feet, he stepped out of his shoes, cords and briefs, the firelight streaking across his magnificent form. He was exquisite, a picture of beauty as he stood above her, his desire evident and bold. Jade reached up her arms to receive him back into her embrace, but he dropped to his knees beside her. His fingers began a languorous journey from the tips of her toes upward, stopping to caress the soft inner warmth of her thighs, the flat plane of her stomach, to find again the luxurious fullness of her breasts.

He settled himself beside her, one muscled leg thrown over both of hers, as he began to explore her body, discovering its mysteries with hands that were followed by lips blazing a trail of heated desire.

As Steve's fingertips found the heated core of Jade's femininity she gasped, writhing under his tantalizing maddening touch. She pressed her hands tighter onto his back, feeling the muscles bunch and move under her palms.

"God, I . . . please, Steve," she said, hardly able to speak.

"Yes. Yes, Jade," he murmured, but still he held back, as if savoring each moment, each memory of her loveliness.

How could such torture be so sweet? Jade ached with a need beyond description, her body arching and moving closer to Steve to bring him to her, to consume her and quell the fire that raged within her.

At last he was there. When she thought she could bear it no longer, he moved over her and came to her in a thrusting force of ecstasy. In matching rhythm they rocked against each other, soaring higher and higher toward the pinnacle that they were seeking.

"Oh, Steve. Steven!" Jade gasped, clinging tightly to him as bright colors danced before her eyes. Then Steve shuddered above her and she felt a sweet fulfillment that she'd never before experienced. He gazed down at her flushed face, his eyes warm and tender, as he brushed a kiss across her lips. Neither spoke nor moved; they simply looked at one another, storing the memory of their lovemaking in secret places in their minds.

"You were wonderful, Jade," Steve said.

"I have never experienced anything so...I...oh, Steve, it was beautiful."

"Jade, I wanted you so much. I'll never get enough of you. You are the most incredible woman I have ever known."

Jade smiled. Her throat had tightened with emotion and the words would not come, so she just smiled. The lovely expression brought the reward of Steve's lingering kiss, and she felt his manhood stir within her as his passion was rekindled. And then she was joining him, marveling at the intensity of their need after having been satiated just moments before.

Again Steve took Jade to just within the sphere of imminent bliss and then joined her to reach the summit in a glorious maelstrom of exploding senses. Jade drifted back in a euphoric state as Steve rolled to his side and then pulled her close to his chest. A fine film of perspiration glistened over their bodies as they lay spent, heartbeats quieting as their breathing returned to normal. Steve stroked her hair in a steady gentle motion, and Jade feared if she didn't move she would fall asleep.

"Oh my," she said, "I feel so..." Words failed her, and she fell silent again.

"Jade, you're not sorry about this, are you? I realize we haven't known each other very long, but—"

"I have no regrets, Steve. There aren't timetables for these things. It's as though you have been a part of my life for an immeasurable length of time. It was right, and good, and...wonderful. I am very, very glad I found you 'dead' under my tree."

Steve chuckled and kissed her on the forehead, and they lay still again for several minutes, the only sound in the room the soothing crackle of the fire.

"Jade," Steve said finally, "spend the night with me. I want to reach out and know you're beside me and make love to you in the morning."

Dangerous. Very dangerous. It was one thing to make love in front of a fireplace, quite another to sleep an entire night in a man's bed. It was too personal, possessive. Jade would be granted yet another glimpse of Steve, see his personal items on his dresser top, sing in his shower, wrap herself in his towel. What if she didn't want to go home when dawn came? What then? How far could she go in this relationship before she could be unable to retain control of her emotions? She was *not* going to fall in love with Steven Robert Chastain. She had to carefully view each new step before she plunged ahead.

She was doing fine, she told herself, was in charge and organized. She had gone to Steve willingly, given of herself and received more than she had ever imagined possible. Now they could continue to see each other daily, enjoy the project of Emma's letters, laugh and talk, knowing the sexual tension that would build over the hours would find release when they came together at day's end.

But Jade had to be careful. She was vulnerable and alone right now and must not allow herself to be swept up in a temporary world by Steve, to be sheltered and held safely in his protecting arms. For it *was* temporary. When Steve returned to his fast and frantic existence, Jade would bid him a quiet farewell. There would be no broken heart, no tears or bitterness. She simply would not allow things to get out of hand while they were together. A practical workable plan *if* she didn't make any mistakes.

"Jade, will you stay?"

"I don't think that's a good idea."

"Why not?"

Why not? Damn it, she had to say something. She couldn't remain here for the night! "I . . . don't have a toothbrush," she said. That was it? That was the full extent of her sophisticated logical reasoning, why she had no intention of spending the next hours in this man's bed? The lack of a toothbrush?

"There are a half dozen brand-new ones upstairs." Steve chuckled. "Any other problems?"

Could she do it? Sleep next to Steve, go through her morning rituals in his home, and remain emotionally detached? Sure she could, now that she was completely aware of what she was doing and had made the decision in a cool state of mind. Nothing to it. Let someone else fix the coffee for a change. What was the big deal, anyway?

"Nope, no other problems," she said brightly. "Is my reservation confirmed?"

"It is. Could I interest you in a dish of ice cream? I'm hungry."

"Sounds reasonable. Have any root beer?"

"I'm never without it, Jade Sinclair. This is a classy place."

Steve pulled on his cords and then handed Jade his shirt, which she buttoned over her full breasts, the tail hanging to the middle of her thighs. She thought she looked silly. Steve said she was gorgeous, and they headed for the kitchen.

"Ugh," Jade said. "I forgot about this mess. Maybe we should clean up first and then have the ice cream."

"Worry not. Here are two spotless bowls with matching spoons. We're all set."

"How can you stand leaving things strewn all over?" Jade said with a frown.

"It's not hurting anything. I'll get to it eventually. It's a matter of priorities. Dirty dishes are low on my list."

"What's high?"

"Oh, you, sex, ice cream. Stuff like that. And root beer."

"That's quite a combination." Jade laughed.

"So what's on your list, Jade?" Steve asked, as he scooped the dessert into the bowls.

"Power, money, instant recognition wherever I go," Jade said, dramatically covering her heart with her hand.

"You're lying."

"You're right."

"I don't think you know," Steve said, looking at her steadily.

"Could be." She shrugged. "That's enough ice cream for me. You can have the one that looks like a frozen mountain."

"Jade," Steve said quietly, "you're running from yourself."

"What do you mean?" she asked, a frown instantly on her face.

"You're not stopping to get in touch with you, to discover who you are and what you need to make you truly happy. It doesn't fit the picture."

"What picture?"

"The overall view you present. You come across as efficient, intelligent, organized to the hilt, and capable of taking care of anything. Except one thing, Jade. You. You got lost in the shuffle in the world you created for yourself."

"For heaven's sake," Jade snapped, "you're doing your shrink number again. I happen to know who I am, Steve. You make me sound like a lamebrain."

"Of course you're not. That's the point. You're too smart not to realize what you're doing. It's one thing to take a vacation, but quite another to simply phase out entirely because you don't know where to go next."

"That's insulting!"

"No, damn it, it's true! How long are you going to sit in Granny's cabin, Jade? Months? Years? All under the pretense that you weren't needed anywhere else anyway? You're feeling sorry for yourself because you've fine-tuned a business to the point that it runs smoothly without you. You have a talent, a gift, and you're viewing it as a disease! It's time to move on to something new. You can't just stagnate!"

"Since when are you my keeper?" Jade said, slamming her bowl on the table. "I really don't remember asking you for your advice, Mr. Chastain."

"It comes free with the ice cream," he said, grinning at her.

"Well, you can keep them both!" she said, spinning around and marching from the room.

Not the most mature performance of her life, but she felt better for having done it, Jade decided, as she stood staring into the fire. Lord, Steve had nerve. The very idea of implying she was practically throwing her life away. What did he know? He had a big fancy career that would keep him busy until he retired. A person didn't pop out of bed one morning and decide on a new life's work. It took time, planning. Why shouldn't she have a nice vacation, for Pete's sake? Because... because she wasn't on a vacation.

Steve was right. Damn it, the rat was right. Jade had fled from Detroit to seek solace at Granny's cabin and had no idea when she would leave or where she might go. But she didn't want to think about it now. Not tonight. Not after the exquisite lovemaking she had shared with Steve. Why did he have to open his big mouth? She'd face her dilemma later, but damn it, Steven Robert, not tonight!

"Your ice cream is melting," Steve said, holding out her bowl.

"Thank you."

"I didn't mean to upset you, Jade. I care very much about what happens to you. I want to help if I can."

"I'm sorry I threw such a fit. I guess I didn't want to hear what I knew was the truth. It's safe here in Dunrovin. I need that for a while."

"I understand. That's why I'm here, too, but I know what I'm going back to."

"I'll figure this out."

"You're not alone, Jade. I'm right beside you."

What an absolutely lovely thing to say! Unexpected tears sprang to Jade's eyes and she blinked them away. Steve Chastain just didn't quit! When she thought she had seen every possible facet of his personality, he came up with another one. Now there he was, offering his support, a rock she could lean against when she grew weary in her struggle to find a new purpose to her existence.

"Oops. Forgot your root beer," he said, striding from the room.

Jade laughed, the lilting resonance echoing through the large room. One minute he had her crying, and the next . . . goodness, Steve was confusing.

"Your brew, madam," he said, returning to the room.

"Thank you," she answered, settling back down on the floor.

Steve sat beside her and they made short work of their ice cream. No, Steve said firmly, she could not carry the bowls to the kitchen. Jade debated the point and was silenced by a searing kiss that erased any thought of dishes and spoons.

"Oh, Jade," Steve said, circling her shoulders with his arm and pulling her close, "do you think life was any simpler back in Emma's day?"

"Probably not to the people living then. Everything is relative to the era."

"I suppose you're right."

"Emma didn't have it so tough," Jade reminded him. "She had homemade ice cream at her birthday party."

"'Tis true. Jade, I do love to hear the sound of your laughter. You've officially christened my new home. I think I'll put up a sign that says 'Jade Sinclair Laughed Here.'"

"And made love here?"

"No way. Can't say that in case Mrs. Steinberg drops by to give me a sermon on my decadent soul."

"She's weird."

"You're right. Hey, listen to that wind hollering out there. Must be another storm coming in. But it doesn't matter, because we're snug and warm. More than that, we're together. Nice, huh?"

"Nice. I like you, Steve Chastain."

"And I like you, Jade Sinclair. Let's go upstairs and make beautiful love together through the night."

The wind continued to whistle through the trees, and a torrent of rain began to beat against the bedroom window as if seeking entry to the warm haven within. But Jade was oblivious to the weather as she was carried again and again to that special place so newly discovered. Steve took her there, and Steve brought her safely back. Later they slept lying close together, hands resting possessively, comfortably on one another. Jade's hair spread out over the pillow in a golden halo, and next to her was a head of dark curls. Once in the night she stirred, and Steve unconsciously tightened his hold on her slender form. She settled back into a peaceful sleep, not waking again until the dawn streaked its fingers of light across the room.

Jade stretched leisurely and opened her eyes, not at all sure where she was. Steve's bed! she thought, instantly alert. But Steve was not next to her. She swung her feet to the floor and walked toward the bathroom, stopping to glance out the window.

"My God." She gasped as she viewed the scene before her.

Large tree branches and other debris were strewn in every direction. Obviously the storm had been fierce, and Jade shook her head in wonder. Safely held in Steve Chastain's embrace, she had heard nothing but his whispered endearments.

Five

———

Jade?"

"Just got out of the shower, Steve!"

"Open the door, I've got to talk to you."

"What's wrong?" Jade asked, coming out with a towel wrapped around her.

"Ben just came by. The manager of your Midland store has been trying to reach you and finally called him. When you weren't at the cabin, he took a chance and came here."

"Ben knows I spent the night with you?"

"That's not the point. The storm blew in the window at the boutique."

"What!"

"I brought your clothes up," Steve said. "Get dressed and I'll drive you into Midland."

"You don't know how much damage was done?"

"No. Hurry up. We'll grab a quick cup of coffee before we leave," he said, striding from the room.

Good Lord! Jade thought. She had been making mad passionate love while Grandmother's Cottage was being blow to smithereens?

Jade tugged on her clothes and quickly braided her hair into a single plait down her back. In an automatic motion she began to make up the bed, only to stop and shake her head in disgust. One of her stores had been ravaged by a vicious storm and she was worried about hospital corners? Her obsession with neatness was becoming borderline sick!

Steve was dressed in jeans and a burgundy sweater and had just poured two cups of coffee when Jade entered the kitchen.

"Steve, you don't have to drive me into Midland. If you'll just take me over to get my car... What is that dirty look for?"

"I'm going with you," he growled. "Drink this."

"You're charming this morning," Jade said, flopping down on one of the chairs.

"Well, you're insulting me!"

"I am?"

"The woman I care about just received word that one of her boutiques took it in the chops, right? You have no idea how severe the situation is or what you'll find when you get there, right? But I'm supposed to just wave goodbye and stay here scrubbing cemented-on lasagna, right? Wrong! Give me a little credit, Jade. Damn it, you really make me mad."

"Sorry," she said, smiling brightly.

"What's so funny?"

"Your curls bounce when you're angry."

"For God's sake, woman!"

"Drink your coffee, Steve."

"Man," he said, sitting down and grinning at her, "you are a crazy lady."

"Actually, I'm very upset but I'm holding myself in check. If those needlepoint kits got wet, they'll be a total loss."

"Don't you have insurance?"

"Of course, that's not the problem. Each one is an original design done by a commissioned artist. It's not a matter of calling a factory and ordering more. The yarn can easily be replaced, but not the canvases. Then there's the work of the customers themselves. Some leave it there while they're taking instruction, and other pieces are being blocked for framing."

"I get the picture. Don't panic. Maybe it's not as bad as it sounds."

It was worse.

There was a tree in the middle of Grandmother's Cottage. A tree!

"Oh, Jade, thank God you're here!" Beth said, hugging Jade as she stepped from Steve's car. "Would you look at this? No, don't it's awful. Oh, my God, what are we going to do? Why did the stupid designer of this mall put trees along the curb in the first place? Little flowers would have been nice and safe."

"Beth," Jade said, "I'd like you to meet Steve Chastain. Steve, this is Beth Pratt, the manager of what is left of this store."

"Hello, Steve," Beth said. "Don't pay any attention to me. I'm hysterical and I'm babbling."

"For good reason, it would seem," Steve said. "Well, let's have a look around."

The three entered through the door and Jade chewed on her lower lip as she viewed the disaster before her.

Broken glass from the shattered window was strewn everywhere, and several of the rockers where the women sat to work were smashed beneath the limbs of the large tree. The wind had done its damage as it came swirling through the gaping hole, ripping completed canvases from the wall and tossing kits and skeins of yarn in every direction. Everything appeared soggy—the carpet, the supplies, even the countertops.

"Dear God," Jade whispered.

"Easy, babe," Steve said softly, squeezing her hand.

"It looks like a war zone," Jade said, moving tentatively forward. "There's . . . nothing left."

"Oh, Jade," Beth said, bursting into tears.

"Hey, kiddo," Jade said, hugging the woman, who suddenly appeared younger than her forty years, "we're not beat, just a little out of commission. No crying. It's wet enough in here."

"I'm sorry," Beth sniffled. "But, damn, what are we going to do?"

"Evict the tree," Steve said, walking toward the back room. "I'll get on the phone and see who's in charge of storm damage."

"Beth," Jade said, "while Steve is using this line, you go to the phone booth on the corner and call in the clerks. We'll need everyone here. Mary Ellen has teenage boys. See if they are free and want to earn some money. Rita drives a truck sometimes. Ask her to bring it today."

"I'm on my way," Beth said.

After Beth had dashed out the door, Jade took a shaking breath and moved further into the room. She picked up a skein of bright blue yarn and stared at it as it lay wet and limp in her hands. Hot tears stung her eyes and she blinked them away angrily. There was no time for emotions. No time for tears of rage. Everyone would be looking to her for direction and strength. Beth had pulled herself together the minute Jade had taken charge of the situation, and the others would expect the same of her. Jade would make things all right again, they would say. Ask Jade, she'll known what to do. She always does. After all, Jade is so organized.

But what about Jade Sinclair? Who did she lean on and turn to for the answers? No one. She was alone, with people counting on her for their futures. She didn't have the luxury of crumbling into a weeping heap or throwing up her hands in defeat. She had to carry on in a cool efficient manner, setting the mood for the others and making decisions that left no margin for error.

God, she was tired. Not physically, but emotionally. She had thrived on this type of power and command of others' destinies. She had viewed it as a stimulating challenge, made promises to people and always kept them, not rested until the goal was achieved. She had needed no one but herself, and had stood alone to bask in the glory of her accomplishments.

But Jade felt different now, changed. She didn't want to be all things to all people, the commander in chief, the steadying force that would take charge and right the wrongs. She needed someone to lean on, someone who would allow her to weep, regain her strength before tackling what she must do. God, what was wrong with her? She should view this storm as a godsend, allow it to serve a purpose by offering her a challenge in her empty existence. Why was she reacting so strangely?

"Jade?" Steve said, startling her out of her reverie. "I finally got through. They'll have a crew out here as soon as possible. I need to call the manager of the mall and have him board up the window. Do you have his number?''

"It's in the leather book on my desk."

"Okay. Are you all right?"

"Yes, I'm fine. Steve, thank you for your help."

"Hey, that's what it's all about, babe. I told you, you're not alone anymore. I'll be back in a minute and we'll get started on this mess."

"Yes."

Jade stood perfectly still until Steve had returned to the back room, his words echoing through her mind. And then there it was, as clear as day. She had not wanted to step back into her old role of the ever-efficient, independent, organized Jade Sinclair because now she subconsciously saw herself as one of a pair, a half of a partnership, a section of a whole. She was...in love with Steve Chastain.

Oh Lord, how had it happened? At what point had she lost control of her emotions? When they made love? When he smiled at her? When he brought her a root beer to go with her ice cream? When? What difference did it make? The fact remained that she had made the biggest mistake of her life. She was hopelessly in love with him. Well, that was just ducky! When she blew it, she really did it up royally. Now, on top of everything else, she had ordered herself a custom-made broken heart! Steve would return to his world and leave her with nothing but memories and an empty bed. Wonderful.

"All set," Steve said.

"Good," Jade said, forcing a smile.

"Where's Beth?"

"I sent her to call the other employees and ask them to come in. We'll just toss out the wet yarn and take inventory later of what we need to reorder. The kits will have to be logged so I know what artists to contact for replacements. There's a record book of which customers had their work here. I'll contact each of them and offer to replace what they lost with something new."

"Want me to phone your insurance agent?"

"God, I never even thought of that!"

"Don't look so stricken," Steve said, smiling. "You can't be expected to do everything, Jade. Is his number in that book?"

"Yes."

"Off I go," Steve said, heading once again to the back room.

Silly man, Jade thought. What did he know? Of course she was expected to do everything. But she wasn't doing it. Steve was there, already taking care of things for her. And she was letting him! As naturally as breathing, she had allowed Steve to enter her exclusive world and take charge of a portion of it. It had seemed comfortable and right. Steve was whipping his part into shape and there stood Jade with a soggy lump of blue yarn in her hands, feeling sorry for herself. Enough. It was time to get to work around there!

"Everyone is on the way," Beth said, bustling in the door.

"Great. Here, have a trash bag. Let's start pitching this yarn." Jade frowned. "This junk sure is smelly when it's wet."

"Jade," Beth whispered, "your Steve is so handsome. He seems awfully nice, too."

"He is, Beth. Steve is special."

"And?"

"And throw the yarn away."

"Well, damn, Jade, I thought you were going to tell me something juicy."

"Nope."

"Jade, I—Hi, Beth," Steve said, coming up on the pair. "Your insurance agent said he'll send you the forms to fill out. I called a glass company and they'll put in a new window tomorrow. I also got a rug-cleaning outfit lined up for the morning to take care of this carpet. What are you two doing?"

"Starting on this stinky yarn," Beth said.

"Let's do it, ladies," Steve said, reaching for a trash bag.

The other employees of Grandmother's Cottage arrived within the next half hour and joined in the project. A short time later a crew of burly men showed up to begin removing the tree, and the store was soon filled with the sound of buzzing chain saws. The trash bags were filled with the damaged yarn and thrown in the back of Rita's truck to be taken to the city dump.

By noon the guilty tree was gone and Steve and Mary Ellen's sons had carted out the remains of the broken chairs. Steve and the boys disappeared, returning with huge sacks of hamburgers and cold sodas, and everyone took a much deserved break to the accompaniment of wooden panels being hammered over the front window.

"So far, so good," Steve said, as they ate leaning against the counter.

"Beth," Jade said, "after lunch call in an order for the yarn and tell them it's a super rush. Oh, and please see if that furniture store has rockers to replace the ones we lost."

Beth nodded. "Got it."

"Then contact the Detroit and Westland stores and have them send up some kits by Air Express."

"Okay."

"The rest of us will divide into pairs and start making a list of the damaged kits before we throw them away."

"Nicely done." Steve smiled. "I'd say you've covered everything."

"Not without a lot of help," Jade said, looking directly into his warm gaze.

"Which is the way it should be," he said quietly.

The afternoon passed quickly as everyone went about their appointed tasks. Jade and Steve worked together, Steve reading the names and numbers of the damaged kits while Jade recorded them on a piece of notebook paper. Rita and Mary Ellen were familiar with the work that belonged to the customers and made a list of those. Beth polished the counters to their original sheen, and the boys completed several trips to the dump in the truck.

"Go home. Rest. I love you guys," Jade said at five o'clock.

"Shall we come in tomorrow?" Beth asked.

"No," Jade said, "I'll meet the carpet cleaners here and start calling the artists and customers. We should be back in business the day after."

"Well, good for us. We make quite a team," Beth said. "Lord, I'm exhausted! Good night, one and all!"

Hugs were exchanged and the weary group made its way out the door. Steve came up behind Jade, sliding his arms around her waist and resting his chin on the top of her head. She leaned back against him, relishing the feel of his hard length supporting her.

"Are you falling asleep?" he asked finally.

"It wouldn't take much. I think I would kill for a bubble bath."

"I'll drive you home."

Jade turned in Steve's arms to gaze up at his handsome face. "How can I ever thank you for what you did today?" she asked.

"You're not understanding it yet, Jade. There was nowhere else I wanted to be. Besides, I got to see you in organized action. You are impressive, my lady. Those people worked hard for you out of respect, not fear. And because you were right in there doing your share."

"So were you."

"But I'm different."

"Why?"

"Because you scare me to death and I figured I'd better do as I was told. I value my life, you know."

"Oh, Steve," Jade said laughing, "you're so funny."

"And you're beautiful, even when your face is dirty."

"I'm grubby all over."

"I'll check."

"No!"

"Have you ever been kissed in Grandmother's Cottage, Jade?"

"Can't say that I have."

"Then log this in as a new experience," he said, claiming her mouth in a long powerful kiss.

"My!" Jade said breathlessly, when he at last lifted his head. "I'll log that in not just as new, but as splendid."

"Good. Now let's go. Your bubble bath awaits you in Dunrovin."

The steady hum of the engine of Steve's car was Jade's undoing, and she leaned her head back and fell asleep within minutes after leaving the store. She made no attempt to struggle against the fatigue as it claimed her, for to stay awake was to think and she would be forced to face the realism of her love for Steve. She simply couldn't deal with it now, not now. Later she would figure it out and decide what she must do. When she wasn't so tired.

"Hey, Sleeping Beauty," Steve said, brushing his lips over Jade's, "you're home."

"Are you Prince Charming?" Jade teased, as she opened her eyes.

"In the flesh. I'll check your cabin over to make sure there's no damage from the storm, and then I'm heading for my own shower."

"I could fix us some dinner," Jade said, getting out of the car. She was acutely aware that she did not want Steve to leave, and she frowned as the truth hit her. She was head over heels in love with a man she'd met on vacation. It should have been a brief romantic interlude by the lake, but she had gone and lost control of her emotions.

"I'll finish up the lasagna when I get to my place," Steve said. "You're beat, Jade. You'll probably fall asleep in the bathtub."

Granny's cabin had suffered no adverse effects from the violent storm, and after kissing Jade several times, Steve slid behind the wheel of the sports car and roared away in a cloud of dust. Jade decided she had better not risk drowning in the tub and instead stood under the shower head and shampooed her hair. Clad in her flannel nightie, she ate a bowl of soup, amazed herself by not cleaning up after the meal, and crawled into bed where she fell asleep instantly.

Jade heard nothing from Steve the next morning before she drove into Midland to meet the rug cleaner at

Grandmother's Cottage. She spent the remainder of the day on the telephone at the boutique, contacting the artists for new kits and soothing upset customers whose work had been destroyed in the storm. It was after eight o'clock that night when she returned to the cabin and she let out a weary sigh. Everything was once more under control. The order of yarn and the kits from the other two stores had arrived, and Beth could open tomorrow with business as usual.

Yes, everything was under control except Jade herself. During the day, the image of Steve Chastain had crept to the front of her mind with alarming regularity. She had seemed to hear his voice and laughter and smelled his after-shave. Desire had stirred within her at the memory of his touch. God, how she loved him. It was beyond description in its intensity and depth. For the first time in her life, Jade was in a situation over which she had no power or command. She could plan and plot and organize to her heart's content, and it would still not bring her Steve's returned love.

Steve was the smart one. He was keeping their relationship in its proper perspective. He knew it for what it was—a temporary joining of two people who would soon go their separate ways. *He* wouldn't ache for Jade when it was over. *He* wouldn't toss and turn through the long nights wishing she were beside him. Steve had entered into a brief pleasurable affair and would walk away unscarred, which he had every right to do. But Jade? She'd never, ever be the same again.

After a tasteless dinner of the leftover soup, Jade cleaned the kitchen, lit a fire in the hearth and sank onto Granny's rocker. An instant later the ringing of the telephone brought her quickly to her feet and rushing to answer it.

"Miss Sinclair? Mr. Chastain here."

"Indeed?"

"Indeed. Too tired for company?"

"No."

"Good. Bye."

Jade laughed as she replaced the receiver. That was what she would call a nice precise conversation. The best part was, Steve was on his way! Jade quickly pulled loose her braid and brushed her hair vigorously until it shone in a golden cascade down her back. The very thought of Steve brought a smile to her lips, but the knowledge that their time together was short caused an ache in her heart.

"Hello, Ms. Executive," Steve said, after coming into the living room and kissing Jade. "Everything ship-shape at Grandmother's Cottage?"

"Enough to reopen."

"I knew you'd be busy all day and there wasn't any point in going in with you, so I went fishing."

"Catch anything?"

"Nope, but it was very relaxing," Steve said, sitting on the sofa and pulling Jade down next to him. "I may retire and lay around and get fat."

"Oh, really?" Jade laughed.

"Sure. You can open another boutique and support me in the manner to which I've become accustomed."

"No way, Chastain."

"Damn. I thought it was a great plan. Guess I'll have to go back to work."

"When?" Jade said quietly, knowing she really didn't want to hear the answer.

"I don't know." He shrugged. "Soon. Say, we owe ourselves two of Emma's letters."

"That's right! I'll bring them out here."

They carefully deciphered the cramped handwriting and then Jade shook her head and frowned. "So that's where Charles is," she said.

"He caught the gold fever," Steve said, "and went off to make a bundle."

"Don't you think Emma came across as a nag? I mean, she went on and on about his foolish notion and how she was praying he'd come to his senses."

"Not what you would call highly supportive." Steve chuckled. "Sounds like Emma knew how she wanted things to be and Charles's independent action didn't sit too well with her."

"You're saying she organized everything?" Jade said, looking up at Steve with a deep scowl on her face.

"Maybe, which is fine if you're single and responsible only for yourself. It's when you start trying to push other people's buttons that the trouble starts."

"Are you trying to tell me something here?" Jade asked tightly.

"You? No, we're talking about Emma. Hey, I want you to know that I have the cleanest kitchen in Dunrovin. I also have dishpan hands."

"Poor baby," Jade laughed. "Would you like a brandy?"

"If you're having one."

She felt as if she needed six brandies! Jade decided, as she went to pour the drinks. Had Steve really been referring to Emma when he spoke of controlling other people's lives, or to Jade? Was that how he viewed Jade? As a button pusher, a manipulator? He certainly enjoyed her company, but was he saying that as a partner in life he wouldn't touch her with a ten-foot pole? Or was she overreacting, reading more into what he had said than was really there? Perhaps he *was* thinking of Emma, but then again...

"You look pensive," Steve said, as she handed him the snifter and settled back down beside him.

"I was just sorting through some things in my mind. You know, Steve, Beth Pratt is a very competent woman. If for some reason she had been unable to locate me, she would have handled that situation at the boutique just fine. Yet, when I showed up—"

"She fell apart. That's perfectly natural, Jade. In a moment of crisis we look to the stronger person, the one who is willing to take the responsibility."

"I did it, too, Steve. You did things I hadn't thought of yet and I was very willing to allow you to take them over."

"Was it painful?" he said with a smile. "Oh, Jade, quit being so rough on yourself. For some reason you believe that anything less than one hundred percent is zero. There is such a thing as compromise, a middle ground. If you don't wash these two snifters tonight, you won't have a filthy kitchen. You'll simply have a couple of glasses on the counter that will need cleaning at some point."

"What has my kitchen got to do with anything?"

"You run your life the same way! I watched you at the shop, Jade. Every time one of us filled a trash bag you looked to make sure we had sealed it correctly."

"I did?"

"Oh, yes. Beth is the manager of that store, but you double-checked her yarn order. You even ran your hand over the counter to make sure she had polished it enough. You asked those boys three times if they knew the way to the dump and—"

"All right, that's enough," Jade said, exasperation evident in her voice as she got up and walked to the fireplace, where she stared into the flames.

"When we made love, Jade, it was beautiful. Do you know why? Because you let yourself go. You came to me with an abandonment I wouldn't have dreamed possible. You didn't analyze it to death or try to control the situation; you gave, totally gave, of yourself. Consequently, you received that type of giving in return."

"What are you saying?" Jade said, spinning around. "I should spend my life in bed making wild passionate love and forget about everything else?"

"Damn it, Jade, quit looking for a fight. You said yourself that you're not totally content with your life. I'm only trying to point out a few things to you that might help you understand how you get yourself backed into the corners you do. If I didn't care about you, I wouldn't bother. Is it so tough, Jade, to reach out your hand to someone? Especially when that person is me? I was your friend before I was your lover. I'd like to think I'm both now."

"I thought friends accept each other just the way they are!"

"That's true. I seem to remember, however, that you were the one who voiced dissatisfaction over the way your life was going. I'm not picking you apart, Jade, I'm trying to help you, for God's sake!"

"How in the hell am I supposed to change who I have been for twenty-six years?" Jade shouted. "Is it so terrible to want to do things right the first time out? Is that a mortal sin or something? Would I be easier to live with if I didn't do my dishes for a week? My God, Steve, what do you want from me?"

"For you to be happy," he said quietly. "You're the most beautiful, vibrant, most exciting woman I've ever met. It's killing me, Jade, to see that haunting pain in your eyes. I want so desperately to make everything perfect for you and I can't. Only you can do that."

Jade could no longer ignore the concern that was so evident in his voice. Shrugging her shoulders, she said in a quieter voice, "Okay, Steve, let's drop it for now. The last thing I have strength for is a fight."

"Oh, babe, I'm not looking to fight. You're so important to me. I want those big brown eyes dancing with joy. That's all I'm trying to do. That, and lure you back into my bed."

"Lure away, mister. This conversation is wearing out my brain."

"Okay, no more heavy talk. But think about what I said. If you could just lighten up a little, take things slower and easier, you'd have time for you. Quit frowning; I really am going to shut up now."

"I should hope so."

"I do care about you, Jade."

"You must, or you wouldn't waste your time lecturing me. Oh, Steve, I understand what you were saying and I appreciate everything you're trying to do for me. Except for Granny, there has never been anyone who has stopped long enough to care."

"Maybe this is your first time to look up and notice."

"Steve," Jade said. Nothing more, just "Steve." She needed to say his name, hear it echo through the room, to assure herself he was truly there. Steven Robert Chastain, the only man she had ever met who saw past her surface beauty and touched her soul. She loved him more, it seemed, with every passing minute.

"Let me love you, Jade," Steve murmured, before claiming her mouth in a searing kiss.

Jade's sob was muffled against Steve's lips as she leaned against him, circling his neck with her arms to draw closer his heat and strength. He was asking her to give of her body, and she would—with the same abandon and willingness he had spoken of before. What Steve would never know was that she was bringing even more to their lovemaking. She would pass into his tender care the very essence of her being; she did not possess the ability to do less. She loved him, and for Jade it was a sacred commitment. Her vows would be silent, known only to herself, for she would not endanger their remaining time together by declaring aloud her undying love. Steve was there now, and she would cherish each moment like a precious gem.

Steve's lips traveled down the slender column of Jade's neck as his strong hands caressed the fullness of her breasts and sent sparks of desire surging through her body. An urgency seemed to engulf them both as they moved against one another, their kisses feverish and rough.

"I want you, Jade," Steve said, his eyes repeating the message with their smoky haze.

They walked into her bedroom, hastily shedding their own clothing to remove the last barrier standing between them and the ecstasy they sought. Steve swept back the blankets on the bed and they tumbled onto it, Steve lifting Jade over him and bringing her to rest on top of his rugged length. Her breasts crushed against the hard chest, the curly mass of hair stroking the full mounds like dancing fingers. Their lips and tongues met as Steve's hands roamed over the soft contours of Jade's slender body. His arousal pressed against her, and she relished its announcement of need, rejoiced in her new-found femininity that made this man want her as much as she did him.

Jade trembled as Steve's hands moved along her sides to the throbbing breasts that awaited his sweet attention. He lifted her upward, his mouth finding a rosy bud, and his tongue flicked it and drew it to a taut button within the dark regions of his mouth. Her breathing quickened and her heart raced as he moved to the other one, the soft flesh responding to his tantalizing foray.

"Steve, please." Jade gasped, as her passion grew to immeasurable heights.

In one fluid glorious motion he rolled her over and joined with her, the force of his manhood instantly lifting her away from reality. Every movement of her body matched his in perfect unison as they soared higher. Steve brought her within a breath of the ecstasy she sought and then hesitated as if wanting to savor the thought of what would come. She could bear it no longer and cried out to him to carry her to that private shore. In a burst of splendor as their bodies shuddered against one another, they were there as never before. Wave after wave of sensation swept through Jade, and she clung to Steve as she felt herself floating above time and space.

Holding her safely in a tight embrace, he brought her back. Jade closed her eyes and etched indelibly in her mind the feel of his crushing weight, the heady aroma of his male perspiration, the tightness of his muscled back under her shaking hands. He moved away gently, pulling her to his side and brushing her hair away from her flushed face.

"So beautiful," he whispered. "When we're together like that, Jade, the world disappears. There's only the two of us in the entire universe."

"I know."

Time passed silently for a while. Then Steve spoke.

"I wish I could spend the night here, but I'd better be getting home."

"Why?"

"I'm expecting an early call from L.A. I don't think we want Ben pounding on your door looking for me."

"Oh, I'm sure he's enjoying this whole thing. He certainly knew where to find me the other morning."

"He said we're creating more excitement in Dunrovin than there's been in ages."

"I bet! Mrs. Steinberg is going to wear herself out making the rounds with her latest bulletin on our sinful deeds." Jade laughed.

"I'll see you in the morning," Steve said, kissing her deeply before leaving the bed and reaching for his clothes. "Well, maybe not. I may have to hang around and wait for that call."

"All right. Is there a problem at your business?"

"Possibly. I hope to be able to handle it by phone. We'll see. Good night, Jade," he said, kissing her quickly.

"Night, Steve."

Jade listened until the sound of Steve's car rumbled away into the night, and then with a sigh she wiggled into a comfortable position. She wanted to sleep. She wished only for the soothing oblivion of slumber with no wakeful hours that would force her to think back over the things Steve had said to her.

He now knew, as she did, that her life was a shambles, that she could not continue to drive herself relentlessly to accomplish a goal, only to face the desolation that consumed her when her goal was achieved. The hour for change had come. She would find her place, where she truly belonged, and stake a claim to the inner peace she so desperately sought. Her future would be whatever she made it.

But she would walk through that future alone, without the man she loved. Steve was reaching out a helping hand, had voiced sincere concern for Jade's well-being, had shown through words and actions that he cared. But he had never said he loved her, and the omission of that statement from his whispered endearments brought a chilling ache to Jade's heart as she stared into the darkness.

Six

When Jade had not heard from Steve by noon the next day, she was restless and edgy with boredom. The cabin was spotlessly clean, calls to the three boutiques found everything running smoothly, and Jade had nothing to do. She decided to pay a visit to Ben McKenna with the hope that Mrs. Steinberg would not pop in. Jade simply was not in the mood.

The day was clear and warm, with a slight breeze that rustled the leaves on the trees as Jade strolled leisurely along the dirt road and entered Ben's store.

"'Lo, Jade," Ben said cheerfully. "Want a root beer?"

"Sure," she said, sinking onto one of the rockers.

"Here you are," Ben said, handing her the drink and sitting down opposite her. "Where's Steve today?"

"He's expecting a phone call."

"Oh, I see. Fine boy, that Steve. Granny would be pleased, Jade."

"No, Ben, I don't think she would."

"Mercy, Jade, you know Granny didn't hold to old-fashioned notions. She'd understand that you healthy children—"

"I don't mean that. It's...oh, Ben, I made an awful mistake. I fell in love with Steve! How's that for stupid?"

"Sounds mighty fine to these old ears."

"Not when you consider the fact that Steve doesn't love *me*."

"Now how do you know that?"

"Because he's never said he does."

"Oh, for heaven's sake." Ben cackled merrily. "Is that all?"

"Isn't that enough?" Jade said crossly.

"You young folks take the cake." Ben laughed, smacking his knee with his hand. "I suppose, of course, you told Steve you love *him*?"

"Of course not!"

"He's going to read your mind?"

"I'm certainly not going to tell a man who doesn't love me that I love him, Ben McKenna! I'm not a complete idiot, and I do have some pride, you know."

"Such foolishness," Ben clucked. "I saw the look in that boy's eyes when he was with you. Whatever happened to two people talking to each other? That used to be the way to get things known. Granny would have expected you to state your business to Steve Chastain and then deal with the chips where they fell. You're acting mighty silly, girl."

"I've never been in love before," Jade said miserably. "I guess this is how it affects me."

"You look as cheerful as my basset hound."

"Thanks a bunch!"

"You're welcome. Drink your root beer and then go home and clean a cupboard so you'll feel better. You've always done good thinking when you were straight-enin' and cleanin'."

"And organizing!" Jade said, getting to her feet. "Don't forget that!"

Jade had a deep frown of perturbation on her face as she made her way home. Ben was a dear, but he was definitely showing his age. The very idea that Jade should march right up to Steve and announce that she was head over heels in love with him! That would accomplish nothing more than earning her the Fool of the Year Award. No way. She and Steve had entered into their affair as willing adults who fully realized it was a short-term contract. The fact that Jade had gotten off the emotional track was nothing to brag about and certainly nothing she could share with Steve. She'd bluff her way through the goodbyes, when they came, with a phony smile plastered on her face and then cry without stopping for the next decade or so.

The sight of Steve leaning casually against his car in front of her cabin stopped Jade's thoughts and brought an instant smile to her face. She hurried to greet him.

"Hello," she said. "Been here long?"

"No. I knew you'd show up eventually. Are you free tonight?"

"Sure. Why?"

"Want to fly to L.A. with me?"

"What!"

"Fly as in airplane. L.A. meaning Los Angeles, California." Steve smiled.

"Come in and lie down," Jade said, walking into the cabin. "You're not well."

"I'm serious!" Steve said, sinking onto the sofa. "I have to go out there to straighten out a snag and I thought you could come along. We'll probably return tomorrow night or we can stay over until the next morning. Well?"

Jade shrugged. "Okay."

"Just like that?"

"If you're crazy enough to ask me, then I'm crazy enough to go," she said, laughing.

"I thought I'd have to tie and gag you," Steve said, shaking his head. "I mean, it's a little impulsive, you know."

"It's the new me. When do we leave?"

"I'll be back to pick you up in an hour. We'll take a charter from Midland to Detroit and catch our flight from there," he said, getting up and pulling her close. "I don't think I'm believing this."

"See you in an hour."

"You bet you will," he said, then kissed her quickly and headed for the door. "In fifty-nine minutes, in fact."

It had happened. Jade had lost her mind! Some spring had sprung in her brain and Jade Sinclair was certifiably insane! Why? What had come over her? The man she loved very calmly asks if she'd like to... Wait a minute. That was it. She was in love with Steve Chastain and she was acting totally bonkers.

And, oh God, it felt *good*! She was alive and excited and...and had to pack her clothes, call Ben to say she'd be away so he wouldn't think she was dead in a ditch, and then go whizzing up to the clouds with Steve without a care in the world. Love was delicious.

Ben was delighted with Jade's news and told her to have a wonderful time. Just to keep things interesting, he said, why didn't Jade and Steve send Mrs. Steinberg a postcard? Jade told Ben McKenna to take a nap.

Having no idea what she might be doing on the Coast, Jade selected a variety of clothes. She took a quick shower and dressed in a royal-blue pants suit with a pale-blue silk blouse. Registering another sensation of recklessness, she left her hair loose and streaming down her back in a golden cascade.

When Steve arrived in brown dress pants and a tan shirt, he kissed her hungrily before placing her suitcase in the trunk of the car. He seemed to have a constant smile on his face as they drove into Midland. Jade knew Steve was delighted with her hasty acceptance of his invitation to fly to California, and so was she. She could not remember ever doing anything with such spontaneity. It was nutty and more than absurd, and Jade felt as though a breath of fresh air had danced across her soul, freeing it.

"So what is this snag you spoke of?" she asked pleasantly.

"Gina Tyrone."

"The movie star?"

"Yep."

"What about her?"

"She's one of my clients. I set it up for her to endorse the Gina line of bathing suits, and she's supposed to be modeling the first styles for photographers right now."

"And?"

"She's pulling a tantrum. Says it's too cold and windy on the beach, her hair is getting messed up, all the usual junk. She wants everything moved to an inside studio, but the contract calls for outdoor shots. She's got my people running in circles. No one can handle her."

"Except you."

"How about that?" Steve grinned, wiggling his eyebrows at her.

"Wonderful," Jade muttered.

"Hey, she's a spoiled brat. I'll just calm her down, turn on my nonstop charm and get the job done."

"This ought to be good. What else does she want from you?"

"My body."

"Steven Robert Chastain!"

"She does! She told me herself! She can't have it, though."

"Why not?"

"Because I'm hooked on a luscious cabin-in-the-woods gal with wheat-colored hair, who might shoot me dead if I indulged in Gina's offer."

"Good thinking, Chastain."

"Seriously, Jade, if I was going to sleep with Gina Tyrone I would have done it by now. I never have, never will. Besides, living in the fast lane doesn't mean I carry on with more than one woman at a time. You are my lady, Jade, don't forget that."

For how long? Jade thought miserably. No, she wouldn't think about that now. Nothing was going to spoil this trip. She and Steve were going to have a wonderful time and that was all that mattered. She'd worry about the goodbyes later.

The charter flight from Midland to Detroit was absolutely awful. Jade had never been in such a small plane, and she was sure one wing was falling off. It was! It creaked and wobbled, and Jade held Steve's hand so

tightly he finally offered his other one as a replace-
ment, saying his fingers were turning blue. The 747 they
boarded in Detroit looked like a mansion to Jade, and
she sank into her first-class seat with a sigh of relief, ignoring the amusement in Steve's eyes.

The trip to California took nearly four hours, but the
time passed quickly. Jade and Steve laughed and talked
and she knew her eyes were sparkling. They wrinkled
their noses at the meal they were served but consumed
it down to the last bite. Jade was aware of the ever-so-
friendly smiles Steve was receiving regularly from the
pretty flight attendant, whom Steve was politely ignoring. Jade felt smug and possessive and silently told the
shapely brunette to take a hike. This hunk of stuff was
hers, Jade thought fiercely. Go drool on someone else!

The first streaks of a California sunset were painted
across the sky in muted tones of purple, orange and
yellow when the plane touched down at Los Angeles
International Airport. Steve retrieved their luggage and
helped Jade into a taxi, then rattled off an address to the
driver.

"Where are we going?" Jade asked, as the cab
whipped through the surging traffic.

"My apartment. We'll freshen up, then I'll take you
out for a fancy dinner."

"What about Gina?"

"I'm not taking *her* on tonight. I'll let my office
know I'm in town and I'll meet the crew on the beach
in the morning. Want to come?"

"Yes! I can hardly wait to see you charm the socks
off her highness."

Steve chuckled and pulled Jade close to his side,
kissing her quickly on the lips. Another first! Kissed in
a taxicab! This was getting better by the minute.

The doorman at the high-rise apartment building tipped his hat as Jade and Steve entered the plush lobby and headed for the elevator.

"I've never been kissed in an elevator," Jade said as it lifted them upward.

"You poor, deprived child," Steve said, pulling her close and remedying the situation.

Suddenly the door swished open and two elderly women stepped in, their eyes widening as Steve continued to thoroughly kiss a blushing Jade.

"She'd never been kissed in an elevator before," Steve said to the women when he finally released Jade.

"Oh," they said, nodding as if the explanation were perfectly reasonable.

A bubble of laughter escaped from Jade's lips, and Steve chuckled as he drew her close to his side. One of the women whispered something about "those dear children" as they stepped out of the eleavtor, and Jade dissolved in merriment just as the door closed behind them. Once on Steve's floor, he unlocked an intricately carved wooden door and pushed it open, then stepped back for Jade to enter. He placed their luggage in the tiled entryway.

Jade moved forward slowly, her eyes widening at the sight of the enormous, lavishly decorated room. The furniture was massive and heavy, the upholstery done in warm earth tones, and one entire wall was gleaming floor-to-ceiling windows. The view from the glass panels was spectacular, with the city of Los Angeles spread out in every direction. Having been otherwise occupied in the elevator, Jade had paid no attention to how many floors they had come up, and she turned to Steve questioningly.

"Is this the penthouse, for heaven's sake?" she asked.

"None other. Care for a drink?"

"Yes, please. You certainly go first-class."

"Always," he said quietly, handing her a glass. "Does that surprise you?"

"No, I guess not. I suppose I'm just realizing how different all of this is from the world we've been sharing in Dunrovin."

"Not really, Jade. We're the same people. The surroundings are a little flashier, that's all."

"You can say that again," she said with a smile.

"Hey," he said, pulling her down next to him on the sofa, "I work hard and make big bucks. Why not enjoy it?"

"I thoroughly agree. By the way, who am I supposed to be?"

"Be?"

"How are you going to introduce me to your staff tomorrow?"

"Jade Sinclair comes to mind."

"Who is? Your consultant from Michigan? Mistress? Bodyguard? What?"

"Bodyguard. I like that one. A female bouncer."

"Seriously, Steve, this is a bit awkward."

"And none of their business. Have you ever been kissed in a penthouse?"

"Nope."

"Well," he said, setting their glasses on the coffee table, "I had better take care of that right now."

"You're ever so kind."

Jade Sinclair had now been kissed in a penthouse. Made love in a penthouse. And taken a shower with the man she adored in a penthouse.

Jade and Steve moved through the large master bedroom, getting dressed for their evening out. Jade glanced at Steve often, her body still tingling from the exquisite lovemaking they had shared. It seemed so intimate to be preparing for their date in each other's company. Almost like being married, Jade thought dreamily, as she slipped a burgundy cocktail dress over her head and lifted her hair so Steve could zip it up.

"Lovely," he said, looking over her shoulder at her reflection in the mirror.

"I like what you're wearing, too."

"I haven't put my shirt on yet?"

"I know. I know."

Steve kissed the nape of Jade's neck, sending sparks shooting through her. She turned to run her hands across the curly mass of dark hair on his chest, her lips and tongue following to draw lazy circles over the rock-hard expanse. She heard his sharp intake of breath and looked up to see the desire flickering through his gray eyes.

"You keep that up and we'll never get out of here," he said, his voice husky.

"Doesn't this place have room service?"

"It's an apartment building, not a hotel, and my kitchen is bare except for coffee and a couple of moldy oranges."

"Oh. Well," Jade sighed, "we'd better go to dinner then. Quit standing around half naked."

"Or you'll attack me?"

"You've got it, Chastain."

"Then I think I'll take my pants off." Steve chuckled as he walked to the closet and pulled out a blue silk shirt.

Jade's eyes were riveted on Steve as he drew the sensual material over his chest and buttoned it into place. No wonder women gawked at him everywhere he went. Dressed, he was a gift-wrapped package, enticing them to discover the treasure underneath. Jade knew and loved every inch of that whipcord body, had been the recipient of its strength, power and expertise. Steve Chastain consumed her, heart, mind, body and soul, and she loved him with every fiber of her being.

Steve swiftly knotted a blue-and-gray tie into place, shrugged into his jacket and reached into a drawer for a handkerchief that he pushed into his pocket. He was devastating, and when he turned to Jade and smiled she melted under his gaze.

"Ready?" he said, not seeming to notice the pink flush on her cheeks.

"Yes. Should we call for a taxi?"

"I keep a car here."

"Of course you do." She laughed. "Silly me. You know, your eyes are totally blue now. You wore that shirt on purpose to try and look sexy."

"Did it work?"

"Nope."

"Damn. Let's go eat."

Steve was greeted by name at the restaurant, and they were immediately led to a cozy table. He selected and approved a French wine and then reached across the table and took Jade's hand.

"I'm very glad you came with me, Jade," he said.

"I am too."

"You really surprised me when you agreed to this."

"I rather shocked myself. I had just come from Ben's, where he had informed me I was less than brilliant, and I was really bummed out. When you suggested ... well, I just up and did it."

"And you didn't make my bed before we left for dinner, and—are you ready for this—you hung your towel crooked in the bathroom."

"Me? Never. Guilty of crooked towel hanging? Please, sir, you insult me."

"Oh, Jade, it's so good to see you like this. You're relaxed, happy. I wish I knew that it would last."

"What do you mean?"

"Jade, when you're all wrapped up in your own concerns, I can't get near you. It's as though only half of you is really listening to me. I know you have worries about your future and what you want to do, but when you get that haunted look in your eyes it frightens me. I feel very far away from you and shut out behind an invisible wall. Seeing you like you are now is so wonderful, Jade. You're here, really here, with me."

The arrival of steaming plates of delicious food rescued Jade from having to reply to Steve's softly spoken statement. Somehow he had known all along what she was doing when she'd replied automatically while actually engrossed in her own thoughts. No one had ever figured that out before. And her eyes? What were they, all of a sudden? Neon signs with flashing messages? Jade is happy. Blink. Jade is sad. Blink. Jade is in love with Steven Chastain. Lord! What if Steve could read the depth of her emotions regarding him?

"This steak is perfect," she said brightly. "I didn't realize I was so hungry. You have style, Steve. Greet me in my front yard in Michigan after lunch and take me to dinner in California. Classy."

"I try."

"You succeed. Granny would have loved this."

"You miss her a great deal, don't you?"

"Yes, she was so important to me. But it's time I stood on my own two feet. I used to run to her every time I bottomed out."

"There's nothing wrong with that, Jade. Sometimes I pick up the phone and talk to my father for nothing more than the sound of his voice. It steadies me, makes me take a deep breath before I move on. We all need someone and it's not a show of weakness. You know my wish is for you to be happy, but more than that I want you to share with me when you're not instead of closing up inside yourself."

"I'm used to being alone," Jade said quietly.

"I know that, but you aren't anymore. That's the part you're not understanding."

"But it's only temporary, Steve."

"What are you saying, Jade?" Steve said, his jaw tightening.

"You'll leave Dunrovin and I'll go . . . wherever it is I'm going."

"Is that all this has been to you? A romp in the woods? A vacation fling?"

"Of course not! I'm being realistic."

"And analytical and organized, I suppose," Steve added.

"Facts are facts! We met in a remote place, a world where neither one of us exists on a permanent basis. What would you suggest? I follow you around the country watching you soothe temperamental movie stars? Or better yet, do you want to come sit with me at Grandmother's Cottage and do needlepoint?"

"I just found you, Jade. I sure as hell don't want to lose you!"

"Don't yell. People are staring at us."

"I don't care, damn it! I really resent the idea that you're going to dust me off when—"

"Dust you off? Are you crazy? I love you, Steve Chastain, and I—Oh God, now I've done it."

"What...did you say?" Steve whispered, a slow smile creeping onto his face.

"Nothing. Finish your dinner before it gets cold," Jade said, draining her wineglass.

"You are in love with me?"

"I'd rather not discuss it."

"Jade, I think I've loved you ever since you tried to pick my pocket under the tree."

"What?"

"Or maybe it was when you thought I was the Michigan Murderer and you were going to stick me with that fork."

"Huh?"

"And I was really lost when I found out you liked root beer. Jade, close your mouth. All I'm trying to say is, I love you, Jade Sinclair."

He loved her? Steven Robert Chastain loved her? Well, how about that? That was wonderful! Wasn't it? Sure it was. So what if they came from totally different worlds and Steve traveled constantly and really didn't live anywhere and... Love conquered all, didn't it?

"You love me," Jade said, shaking her head. "I had no idea. I mean..."

"I thought you didn't have room in your life for love, Jade, wouldn't allow yourself to become involved in something so... emotional. I know your need to feel in control of every situation, and love has a way of scrambling brains—or so I've found out since meeting you."

"Tell me about it. I'm sitting here in L.A., remember?"

"You came because you love me?"

"Yes. I had been telling Ben that I love you but that you didn't love me. He said I should tell you how I felt, but that seemed out of the question, and I was so depressed. Then there you were leaning against your car, and now here I am."

"Oh, Jade, this is fantastic! I'm going to order champagne. We're going to celebrate!"

After three glasses, Jade was glowing. The only man she had ever loved was in love with her and life was a joy to behold. When she finished the fourth she was nearly weeping with happiness, and she leaned her head on Steve's chest as he led her out to the dance floor. Old Ben McKenna had been right all along. Yes sir, when you're in love with someone, just open your mouth and let it out. Nothing to it.

Jade hiccuped.

"Excuse me," she mumbled.

"I think you're slightly blitzed." Steve chuckled, causing her head to bob up and down.

"No, I'm just happy," she insisted, but the second hiccup gave her away.

Steve nodded. "Sloshed. Let's go before you fall on your nose."

Jade smiled at everyone she saw—although they all appeared slightly blurry—and then found herself in the front seat of Steve's plush automobile. She hummed for a while, but when Steve started laughing she decided it must not have been his favorite tune.

Her stomach did not appreciate the ride up in the elevator, and Jade groaned. Steve pulled her close to his side and patted her on the head. He kept chuckling about something, but she simply did not have the energy to ask what was so funny.

Suddenly there was a man taking off her dress! "What are you doing?" Jade protested.

"Shhh. It's me, babe, Steve. I'm just going to put you to bed."

"Oh, how lovely," she purred, leaning against him.

"Remind me not to buy you wine and champagne at the same time," he said with a laugh.

"Huh?"

"There you go, all tucked in. I love you, Jade."

"I love you too."

"Good. That's the best news I've had all evening. Sleep well, my Jade Sinclair," he said quietly, kissing her on the forehead.

When Jade stirred and opened her eyes the bedroom was flooded with sunlight and she moaned, her hands flying to her aching head. She must have been mugged, whopped on the bean and... In Dunrovin? Never. Then what... Wait, this wasn't her bed. She'd been drugged and kidnapped and... Slowly the fog was lifting. Los Angeles. Steve. Wine and champagne because they were in love with each other. Glory be, it was true! She had said... Then he had said...

"Good morning," Steve said, striding into the room clad only in tight-fitting jeans. "How are you feeling?"

"Don't ask. I will never, ever drink again."

"That's what they all say. Here, I poured you a cup of coffee at the sound of your first moan of misery."

"Thank you," Jade said, pushing herself up against the pillows. "Good grief, I'm undressed. I don't remember taking off my clothes."

"Oh, really?" Steve said, handing her the cup and sitting down next to her. "Or what came afterward?"

"Afterward?"

"I have to tell you, Jade, you were something. A real wild woman. I've got the bruises to prove it."

"Bruises?" she said, her eyes widening.

"At first I thought, hey, this is a little kinky, but if my lady wants to—"

"Kinky!"

"Don't worry about it," he said, patting her knee. "All the experts say that what you do in the privacy of your own bedroom is perfectly normal."

"What did I do?" Jade demanded.

Steve fell apart. He hooted and hollered and laughed so hard that tears came to his eyes, while Jade stared at him as though he were totally deranged.

"I'm kidding," he said, gasping for breath. "You passed out practically before I got your dress off. I never laid a glove on you."

"You made up all that garbage?"

"You should have seen the look on your face," he said, dissolving again in a fit of laughter.

"You're sick, Chastain!"

"You can't be mad. You love me, remember? And I love you."

"Really? Did I say that? I must have been stoned."

"You can't wiggle out of it, Jade. I recorded the whole conversation."

"What?"

"With my secret recorder ring. See, I saved up these cereal box tops and—"

Suddenly it was Jade's turn to laugh. "I love you, Steven Robert. You're a crazy man, but I do love you."

"And I love you, Jade Sinclair. What's your middle name?"

"Emma."

"You were named after Granny's mother?"

"Yes."

"I like it. Jade Emma Sinclair, you I love. How's your head?"

"Much better. Thanks for the healing brew," she said, placing the cup on the nightstand. "What time are we due on the beach to meet the lovely Miss Gina?"

"Later," he said, slowly pulling the sheet away. "Much later."

"I'm sorry I conked out last night," Jade said breathlessly as Steve's hand traveled up her leg.

"We'll make up for it," he said, leaning forward and placing light kisses over her breast.

"Now?" she gasped, as desire swirled throughout her.

"Oh yes, ma'am, right now."

"There's no time like the present, I always say," Jade said, sliding down off the pillow and circling Steve's neck with her arms.

And it was much, *much* later before Jade stood under the shower, a lovely smile of contentment on her face. Steve had come to her with vehemence that had both startled and delighted her. He had brought Jade quickly to a fever pitch of desire with his questing tongue and stroking hands that seemed everywhere at once. She called to him to quench the shaft of fire that spread throughout her, and Steve had answered her plea with the force of his manhood.

Again and again Steve had declared his love as his voice caressed her name, and then slowly, gently this time, he had rekindled the ember of passion until it burst into the familiar welcome flame.

Steve. Dear, sweet, wonderful Steve, who loved her. The declaration of his innermost feelings seemed to be finally reaching Jade's understanding as the water of the shower beat against her tender breasts, so sensitive now from her exquisite lovemaking with him. A part of her mind was jubilant, happy beyond description, as she realized the elusive dream had come true: the man she loved returned that affection in kind.

Oh, damn, why couldn't she just leave it at that for now, let the bliss of that truth wash over her in a benevolent cloak? Damn her analytical psyche for going further and beginning the questions to which there were no answers.

Only in movies and romance novels did love conquer all, and this was honest-to-goodness life! She and Steve *did* live in different spheres. Jade needed an orderly predictable existence that was preplanned and organized. Though it had ultimately brought her a sense of emptiness at job's end, it was the only way she knew to function. Her madcap flight to Los Angeles had been daring and fun, but it was against every facet of her basic nature. She had to have security, a home, a well-thought-out purpose to her life.

And Steve? He had created a world for himself that was fast and frantic, that took him winging across the country at the mere ringing of a telephone. He had sought out Dunrovin as a temporary haven, but had not hesitated to leave when his career beckoned. He moved in a circle of celebrities with fragile egos and temperaments, and Steve thrived on rushing to the scene to soothe the demanding personalities and bring order to chaos. Home to him was the place of the moment, with no concern for where tomorrow might find him.

How could they mesh, bring even a semblance of compromise to their lives? Jade could never exist flitting from city to city as nothing more than the woman on Steve's arm. Her love for him filled a part of her being, but her person, her individual identity, would crave an outlet for her intelligence and drive. Steve was presently enjoying the low-key solitude of Dunrovin, but it would be foolish to believe he could be content there for any great length of time. He would become restless and bored, eager to get back to the fast-paced existence in which he thrived.

Didn't Steve realize the problems that confronted them? Was he still so exhilarated over the discovery that Jade loved him, that he hadn't stopped to see that their future together was laden with obstacles? Well, more power to him. Let him stay in his euphoric state for now and relish the sensations of loving and being loved in return.

"Jade?" Steve called. "Did you die in there?"

"Coming!"

"I'm starving! Let's go eat breakfast."

"Okay," she agreed, coming out of the bathroom. "What do I wear for the encounter with Gina Tyrone?"

"Jeans. We'll be tramping around on the beach," Steve said, pulling a kelly-green sweater over his head. "Don't say one word about how chilly it is out there. I'm going to convince Gina it's a balmy day in smoggy L.A."

"With your charisma?"

"Of course. We'll stop by my office first so I can check on everything in general, and then go play nurse-maid to Miss Glamorous."

"I've seen her in the movies," Jade said, brushing her hair. "She's really beautiful."

"Yeah, I guess, but I'm not overly fond of people who think they're better than everyone else. I deal with a lot of those. They are a pain in the butt."

"But you enjoy your work, don't you?"

"Sure. It's never dull, that much is for certain. Hurry, put your shoes on. I'm going to pass out from hunger."

Dull, Jade thought, as she followed Steve from the room. He had said the word as though it left a bad taste in his mouth. Steve had gotten in touch with himself long ago and realized his need to be free from a constricting career that would tie him behind a desk. He had worked hard to achieve the lifestyle that offered him the challenge and excitement he craved. Jade respected him greatly for what he had done and for knowing his inner being so well. But where would she fit in? What place could she possibly hope to find in Steve's life? In spite of their mutual love, what would prevent the unavoidable goodbyes in the end?

Seven

—

They ate at a busy restaurant, and then Steve drove through the tangled mass of traffic with the relaxed confidence of one who had done it many times before. He pulled into an underground garage and was greeted by name by the security guard on duty at the elevator. As they stepped out onto the twenty-sixth floor, Jade's eyes swept over the lush reception area that had been decorated in gray, blue and rose.

"Mr. Chastain!" cried the young woman behind the reception desk. "I'm so glad you came back from Michigan. Gina Tyrone is driving everyone crazy. Do you know what she called me when I told her you were away! No, I can't say it. I'm too much of a lady. But now that you're in charge, everything—"

"Hello, Chris," Steve said, chuckling. "Sounds like you've had a rough time. Tell you what. Call the an-

swering service and have them take over and you go
home for the day."

"Really?"

"Yep. Are my messages on my desk?"

"Yes, and thanks a million!"

"You're welcome, Chris. Surprise that nice new
husband of yours and invite him out to lunch."

"I will! Bye."

"Cute girl," Jade commented, as they walked down
a carpeted hallway.

"Good secretary, too. Guess Gina's really on the
warpath. I'll have my hands full."

"Steve!" a male voice bellowed, causing Steve and
Jade to turn as they were descended upon by a tall
handsome blond man who was clad in jeans and a T-
shirt and appeared to be in his early thirties.

"Jade Sinclair, this is Randy Crane, the best pho-
tographer in the business," Steve said. "Randy, this is
Jade. Don't touch her, she's mine."

"Got it, boss. You're gorgeous, Jade. I'd love to
capture that hair on film."

"Thank you," Jade said, laughing.

"Come to my office, Randy," Steve said, opening a
door, "and tell me the bad news."

"There's no dealing with Gina," Randy said, as the
three entered the enormous room. "Hell, I offered her
dinner, my body, everything, but she said no way. She
wants you here and that's that. We were all set up on the
beach and she refused to model the bathing suits. It was
too cold, too windy. You name it, she didn't like it."

"All right," Steve said, sinking into a large leather
chair behind his desk, "go on out there and get ready.
I'll be along to handle her."

"Great. See you later. You coming too, Jade?" Randy asked, heading for the door.

"Wouldn't miss it."

"Oh, man, Gina's gonna throw a fit!" Randy laughed. "This is going to be something to watch!"

"Goodness, Steve." Jade frowned. "Is Gina actually *that* jealous?"

"Don't worry about it. Sit a minute while I look over these messages."

Jade sat on a leather sofa and surveyed the office. It was decorated with masculine flair yet was still comfortable and inviting. Steve looked just right sitting behind the massive hand-carved desk, and Jade had no difficulty picturing him as the leader, the commander in chief of the prestigious firm. There was an aura of power surrounding him that invoked respect when he walked into a room. Jade had seen the admiration on Chris's face, and in spite of Randy's carefree attitude he obviously held Steve in high regard.

Jade watched as Steve frowned and then reached for the telephone on the edge of his desk. He punched in a series of numbers. His voice was crisp as he asked for someone named McPherson, who apparently came immediately on the line.

"Steve Chastain. I got your message. My contract with you is clear. You deliver the sports bags on time or you lose the endorsement."

Put up or shut up, Jade thought merrily.

"Sorry, chum, no extension. What's it going to be?"

I'll get them there, Mr. Chastain, sir, Jade thought, suppressing a giggle.

"I figured you'd see it that way." Steve nodded. "We'll be in touch."

"You're a tough dude," Jade said, as Steve replaced the receiver.

"Ain't I though?" He laughed. "The rest of this can keep. Let's head for the sand and surf."

The sky was overcast and a brisk breeze was blowing, and Jade decided that *she* wouldn't want to be traipsing around on the beach in a skimpy bathing suit. She was anxious to see how Steve would mollify the fuming Gina Tyrone. If anyone could get the temperamental movie star to wiggle her way through the cold Pacific, it would be Steve.

"Brrr," Jade said, as they stepped out of the car in a paved lot above the beach. "The wind off the water is grim."

"Shh, not so loud," Steve said. "When we get down there, start complaining that you're roasting in your sweater and you wish you could go swimming."

"Do I look crazy? All Randy is going to capture on film is Gina's goose bumps."

"She has other attributes." Steve chuckled.

"I bet she does."

A striped canvas tent had been erected on the sand and a half dozen people were milling around, including Randy, who sprinted over to Jade and Steve as they approached.

"Gina's sulking in the tent," Randy said. "I said you were on the way, but she didn't believe me."

"Wonderful," Steve muttered, steering Jade in the direction of the enclosure. "Gina?" he called when they were standing outside the flimsy structure. "It's Steve."

Jade's eyes widened and she took a step backward as a body clad in a silk robe came flying out through the flap and adhered itself to Steve, a mane of brilliant red hair flying in all directions.

"Steve, darling. Oh, my darling," a sultry voice said, "you've come to rescue me from this insanity."

Good Lord! Jade thought. Was she for real!

"Now, now, Gina," Steve said, flashing his most dazzling smile, "surely things aren't that bad."

"Bad?" the star shrieked. "It's horrendous! They expect me to pose for a camera when my teeth are chattering? I refuse! I simply will not do it!"

"Gina," Steve said, patting her on the back, "you know that Randy is good and he's fast. It will all be over before you know it."

"No!"

"Come on, sweetheart, for Steve? I flew all the way from Michigan to see you in those suits, and I can't believe you're going to disappoint me."

"Ha! I seem to remember when you refused a simple request of mine!"

"Gina, flying to Acapulco for the weekend is not a simple request," Steve answered. Jade wiggled her eyebrows at him and was rewarded by his stormy glare.

"Steven, I am not putting on a bathing suit in this weather," Gina said, stamping her foot.

"But—"

"I said no and I mean no!"

"But—"

"And forget turning on your sexy charm because I'm not going to do it!"

"Of course you're not," Jade said, causing Steve and Gina to look up in surprise. "I am."

"What!" Steve and the astonished star gasped in unison.

"How do you do, Miss Tyrone," Jade said, shaking the woman's hand vigorously. "I'm Jade Sinclair. Have you heard of me? No, I suppose not. Well, I'm a model, you see, and I've been asked to be photographed in the Gina bathing suit so you won't have to suffer in this god-awful weather. Wasn't that just too sweet of your Stevie to arrange this for you? He's such a dear. Anyway, if you'll just show me where the suits are, I'll—"

"Who is this creature?" Gina yelled.

"I—," Steve started, only to stop and stare at Jade with his mouth open.

"Like I said, I'm Jade—"

"No one wears the Gina but Gina!" the movie star bellowed. "How could you do this to me, Steve?"

"I—"

"I'll be out in five minutes. You tell Randy to get ready. And get this blond-haired floozy out of my sight!"

"You mean I'm not going to get my picture taken?" Jade wailed.

"Over my dead body, honey," Gina said, flouncing into the tent.

Uh-oh, Jade thought, seeing the tight set to Steve's jaw. She was a dead person.

Steve ran his hand over his eyes and slowly down his face, shaking his head as if not believing what he had just witnessed. Glancing at the tent, he grabbed Jade by the arm and hauled her about twenty feet away as she eyed him warily.

"You," he said, waggling a long finger at her, "you are marvelous! Oh God," he gasped, dissolving in laughter, "I can't stand it! It was brilliant. Absolutely brilliant. You deserve an Academy Award, Jade."

"Lord, for a minute there I thought you were going to punch me in the chops."

"Never," he said, pulling her into his arms. "How did you know what to say to her? I was getting nowhere fast."

"Women understand women, my sweet. I hit on her vanity. You heard her. Only Gina wears the Gina. Pretty smart, huh, Stevie?"

"That part was a little much," he said, grinning. "Stevie?"

"It's cute."

"Not the image I'm trying to invoke."

"Are we rolling?" Randy asked, strolling up to Jade and Steve.

"We are, thanks to Jade," Steve said. "If Gina gives you any trouble, tell her Jade is the hottest new model in town. Got it?"

Randy shrugged. "Whatever."

The photography session went off without a hitch except for the murderous glances Gina Tyrone threw at Jade every few minutes. Jade smiled politely, while Steve's shoulders shook with suppressed laughter. Jade couldn't remember when she'd had so much fun, and she frowned in disappointment when Randy said it was a wrap.

"Come on, Jade," Randy said, running up to where she stood with Steve. "I have half a roll left. I have to get some shots of that gorgeous hair."

"Why not?" Jade said, striking a provocative pose. "Fire away."

As the camera clicked rapidly, Jade looked up to see Steve smiling at her with a warm tender gaze radiating from his eyes. She stopped perfectly still, suddenly held immobile under his mesmerizing stare, as Randy continued to move around her.

"Whew!" Randy finally said. "I can hardly wait to see these."

"What?" Jade said, seeming to come out of a trance. "Oh, thanks, Randy, that was exciting. I feel like a celebrity."

"Let's go," Steve said quietly. "I'll be talking to you soon, Randy. Take Gina out to lunch."

"You're on, boss. See ya, Jade."

Steve maneuvered the automobile through the traffic but did not speak as he drove. Jade looked at him, seeing the serious expression on his face.

"What's wrong?" she asked.

"Nothing. I was just thinking. You were good out there today, Jade. You sized up the situation and acted on it immediately. You have a natural insight into people's personalities."

"It was a lucky shot," she laughed.

"No, it wasn't. Jade, how would you like to work for me?"

"What!"

"I'm serious. I want to hire you as an administrative assistant to handle some of my clients."

"Steve, don't be ridiculous! I don't know anything about promotion."

"But you do understand people, and that's the biggest part of the job. The rest I'll teach you. Well?"

"This is a joke, right?"

"No."

"You'd be my boss?"

"I suppose so. I realize you're used to running your own show, but once you learned the ropes you'd be pretty much on your own. Hey, I pay good, and think of the fringe benefits you'd get."

"Fringe benefits?"

"Me! I'd break my own rule about never fraternizing with my employees. We'd be a great team, Jade, in more ways than one."

"But where would I live? I mean, you move all over the place."

"Pick a spot. Here? Detroit? Houston? I'll set you up in any one of my offices you choose."

"But where would *you* be, Steve?"

"With you as much as possible. Say yes, Jade."

"I...I don't know what to think! You've really taken me by surprise here."

"Promise me you'll toss it around in your mind?"

"Yes. Yes, of course I will."

"Great. How about seafood for lunch? I know a terrific place."

"Fine."

At the restaurant Jade excused herself to go to the ladies' room, her mind whirling from what Steve had proposed. Work for Steve? For the first time in her life be accountable to a boss? Said person being her lover? It did not sound like the best plan in the world. Yes sir, Mr. Chastain. Right away, Mr. Chastain. Anything you say, Mr. Chastain. Ugh. But then again, Steve had said she would be pretty much on her own once she learned the ropes. From what Jade had seen today the promotion business *was* fun and exciting. And she and Steve *would* be together. Together. What a glorious word. Jade wouldn't exactly be throwing aside her own plans to take this on. Hell, she didn't have any! No, now wait. She had to give this more thought, think it through completely and cover every minute detail in her mind. She couldn't just go off half-cocked.

"I'll do it," Jade said, as she slid into the booth across from Steve. "I'll work for you."

"Jade, that's wonderful! Oh, babe, this is going to be fantastic. You'll never be bored, I can guarantee you that. Do you want to work out of the Detroit office, or where?"

"Yes, I think that would be best. That way I can keep in touch with the boutiques and be able to go to Dunrovin and... You'll be coming to the lake, won't you?"

"Of course. I didn't build that house to sit empty for months at a stretch. Let's get a flight back to Detroit tonight so I can start showing you around your new office tomorrow. Oh, Jade, I am so glad you agreed to this. You'll have a challenge in your life, I'll get a top-notch assistant, and we'll be sharing it all. It's perfect."

"Perfect," Jade agreed. Then why was there that niggling doubt in the pit of her stomach? That inner voice whispering to her to stop and take a good long look at what she was doing. Something just wasn't right, but what?

Back at Steve's apartment he called the airlines and booked them on a four o'clock flight to Detroit. He continually pulled Jade into his arms and kissed her, telling her how happy he was over her decision to join him in his world. His enthusiasm was infectious, and Jade soon pushed aside her lingering doubts and let her excitement for the new adventure take over. One particularly searing kiss brought them tumbling onto the bed. They hastily removed each other's clothing and came together in an ecstasy-filled union that resulted in their nearly missing the plane.

During the trip, Steve explained that Jade's first client would be a member of the Detroit Lions football team, who had just signed a promotion contract with Steve's firm. Jade would be supplied with files showing what ideas had already been used for sports figures, but Steve was sure she would be able to come up with some innovative schemes. Her suggestions would be screened by Steve, and then Jade could present them to the athlete on her own. When he had made his selection, she would contact manufacturers and convince one of them that a football star's endorsement would be perfect for their product. Once all contracts were signed, Jade would be responsible for the client through the entire production of the commercial, or catalog photography, or whatever it was she had set up.

"Got it?" Steve concluded.

"It sounds as though I'm practically going to be living with this jock," Jade said with a laugh.

"Bear in mind, sweet Jade, that you are mine!" Steve said, kissing her deeply.

Another first. Jade had now been kissed on an airplane.

Steve's apartment in Detroit was again the penthouse of a high-rise building in an exclusive section of the city. They dined at a fashionable restaurant, where Steve said any more discussion of business that night was strictly taboo. Tomorrow would be soon enough, he said firmly, for Jade to get a further glimpse of her new career.

Their lovemaking that night was slow and tender, and Jade's mind was filled with only one thought. She loved Steve Chastain and he loved her, and everything was absolutely fantastic! Yet, when Steve gave in to the fatigue that claimed him, Jade lay beside him, listening to his steady breathing and staring up into the darkness with a frown on her face.

Everything had happened so quickly. It was so against the orderly precise manner which she used to plan her life. But it was too late now. She had committed herself to working for Steve and she would honor that agreement. But it was more than that and Jade knew it. She had seen a way to be with the man she loved and she had grabbed it with no hesitation. Well, the die was cast, and she'd worry about her rash actions later.

Jade snuggled closer to Steve's sleeping form and relished his strength, the heat emanating from his body. A comforting realization brought her the soothing oblivion of sleep. She was no longer alone.

The next morning, Jade insisted that Steve take her to her apartment for clean clothes and he agreed immediately, stating he was curious to see her humble abode.

"Forget humble," Steve said, after whistling low and long when they entered Jade's living room. "This is sharp."

"Thank you, sir," Jade said, her gaze following his as he surveyed the tasteful furniture done in delicate shades of mint green and pale yellow. "I'll change and be right out."

"Jade, you've been awfully quiet this morning. Is anything wrong?"

"No, I guess I'm just a little nervous. It's not every day a girl starts a new job."

"But you have such a congenial boss," he said with a grin, "so there's nothing to worry about."

"We'll see," she said, heading for the bedroom. "You're probably an ogre."

"Me? Never."

Since Steve had dressed in a dark business suit, Jade selected a pale-blue linen dress with simple lines and twisted her hair into a chignon at the base of her neck.

Party time was over. The occasion called for the cool professional image she was accustomed to presenting. The Jade with the cascading golden hair and tight jeans would be placed on the back burner for a while.

"You look like a real executive," Steve said, when Jade reentered the living room. "Very nice, but I miss seeing your hair already."

"What goes up can always come down," Jade said, batting her eyelashes at him.

"Tonight," he murmured, close to her lips. "I'll see it tumbling over my pillow tonight."

"Hold that thought," Jade said breathlessly. "We'll conduct an in-depth discussion on it . . . later."

"I love you, Jade," Steve said, and took possession of her mouth in a long powerful kiss.

The Detroit branch of Steve's firm was housed in an office twenty-four floors above the ground in the downtown business district, and the reception area had been decorated in the same colors as the one in Los Angeles. The secretary who greeted them was a thin woman in her fifties who was dressed in a severe tailored suit and spoke in a crispy efficient manner, informing Mr. Chastain that he had a stack of phone messages waiting for him on his desk.

"Thank you, Suzanne," Steve said. "I'd like you to meet Jade Sinclair, my new administrative assistant. Jade, this is Suzanne Kaplan, who keeps this place running like a finely tuned machine."

"Miss Sinclair." Suzanne nodded. "I am at your disposal."

"Thank you, Suzanne, but please call me Jade."

"Yes, of course, Jade. Would you two care for coffee?"

"No, thanks," Steve said, "we just had breakfast. Come on, Jade, I'll show you your office."

"Doesn't Suzanne ever smile?" Jade whispered, as they walked down a carpeted corridor.

"Rarely, but she's a very nice lady and highly efficient. You'll get along fine."

"She didn't seem thrilled to see me."

"She'll warm up once she gets to know you. Here you are," Steve said, pushing open a door.

"Oh, it's lovely," Jade said, entering the large room that was done in cool shades of pale-blue and gray. The windows afforded a view of the rippling waters of the Detroit River and the Canadian skyline on the opposite shore.

"You can have it redone if you like," Steve said. "Fix it to suit your own taste."

"It has a woman's touch."

"It belonged to a gal who left me to stay home with newborn twins. The office across the hall is Mike Pearson's. Forty-five, married, three kids, and presently in Alaska filming a fish stick commercial with a child actor and some Eskimos."

"Alaska!"

"Yep. The other office is empty and used by people who fly in from L.A. and Houston. Randy will pop in and out because I prefer him over the rest of the photographers. Your private bathroom is in there. There's an intercom system connecting you to me and Suzanne, and she will screen all your calls and visitors so you aren't disturbed unnecessarily. Feel free to make any and all long-distance calls. It's faster than letters and adds a personal touch. Contracts are drawn up by a staff of lawyers, so you're not responsible for the fine print. Any questions?"

"How long a lunch break do I get?" Jade smiled, trying to ignore the wave of apprehension that swept over her at the brusque impersonal tone of Steve's voice as he had recited his dissertation.

"Some days we do well to grab a quick doughnut," he said absently, striding from the room. "Follow me. I'll show you my inner sanctum."

Steve's office was enormous and lavishly furnished, but Jade hardly noticed as she walked to the window while Steve shuffled through the stack of messages on his desk. She was suddenly overwhelmed by the magnitude of her hasty decision to work for Steve. She had embarked on a career she knew absolutely nothing about, and answered to a man who obviously said things once and expected his directives to be carried out to perfection. She was used to giving orders, not receiving them, and had not cared one bit for the business-like attitude Steve had adopted in her office.

God, what was she doing there!

"Jade," Steve said, snapping her out of her reverie, "why don't we take a charter to Midland this afternoon and get your cabin and my house closed up. We can drive back tomorrow and you can report in here the day after."

"Yes, all right. I'll need my car."

"I want you to ride back with me. I'll make arrangements to have your car brought down."

"But—"

"Suzanne," Steve said into the intercom, "please book a charter for Midland as soon as possible."

"Right away, Mr. Chastain," Suzanne's voice answered.

"And Suzanne?" he said. "Tomorrow pull every file we've got on sports-oriented clients and put them on

Jade's desk for her review. Also get her the bio on Buffy Phillips. He'll be Jade's client."

"Yes, sir."

"So," Steve said, coming up behind Jade and circling her waist with his arms, "how do you like your new home away from home?"

Jade leaned back into the hard length of Steve's body and closed her eyes, drinking in her fill of his whipcord strength, his familiar male aroma. God, he felt good. There in his arms she felt safe, protected and instantly cloaked in a blissful contentment. Held securely in the embrace of that one special person, everything seemed to fall perfectly into place. There were no problems or inner anxieties, there was only Steve.

"Jade?"

"I'm very happy, Steve," she said quietly.

"Me too, my love."

The charter flight from Detroit to Midland was as gruesome as it had been the first time, and Jade sank gratefully into the front seat of Steve's car after leaving the small aircraft. Granny's cabin looked cozy and inviting when Steve unlocked the front door and set Jade's suitcase inside.

"You are beat," he said, pulling her close. "I'll get out of your way and let you get to bed early."

"Alone? Sounds dull."

"Definitely will be, but I'll pick you up at nine in the morning and we'll head back to the big city. Can you take care of everything by then?"

"Yes. I'll just pack up the perishable goods and give them to Ben. He always keeps an eye on the cabin when I'm not here."

"Good. Night, Jade," he said, kissing her long and hard before leaving and closing the door quietly behind him.

Jade sank onto the rocker by the fireplace, suddenly so tired she felt as if she could not move a muscle in her body. Had it only been a few days since she had left the sanctuary of this cabin? It seemed like weeks. Jade was changed, different. She was…loved. Loved by the only man who had ever invoked the turbulent emotion within her.

But more than that had changed! In her fear that she was destined to lose Steve after all, she had made a major decision regarding her career. She had never before done anything so rash. She didn't want to work for Steve—or anyone else, for that matter. *She* controlled the situations she tackled. Jade Sinclair called the shots and issued the orders. Doughnut for lunch? Ha! She'd eat when and for how long she chose, by God! No curly-haired hunk of man was going to tell her what she was going to do!

"Yes, he is," Jade said miserably. "He's the boss. How did I get myself into this mess?" Well, what was done was done. She'd take on the Gina Tyrones and the Buffy Phillipses and do a fantastic job of it. Buffy? God, what a name for a football player. How could she promote a big dumb jock with a handle like Buffy? Buffy Beer? Buffy Bedspreads? Buffy Birdbaths?

A giggle escaped from Jade's lips and she pushed herself out of the rocker with a smile on her face. In a renewed burst of energy she packed her luggage for the return to Detroit and set out a box to fill in the morning with food from the refrigerator. Moving through the cabin, she collected her personal items, her travels bringing her to the second bedroom and the stack of Emma's letters enclosed in the plastic folders.

Jade hesitated in the doorway, realizing that if she spent the remaining hours of the evening deciphering the cramped handwriting, she could no doubt finish the project and perhaps solve the mystery surrounding Emma, Charles and Henry. But no, she had promised Steve she wouldn't look at the letters until he was with her to share what they would discover. Emma would simply have to wait until Jade and Steve came back to Dunrovin for a weekend of peace and quiet. Whenever that would be!

Jade carefully placed the precious dispatches in the trunk and closed the lid. Charles was off panning for gold, Emma was not happy about the situation, and Henry had yet to arrive on the scene. It was worse than missing an installment of a soap opera!

After a bacon-and-eggs dinner, Jade thoroughly cleaned the cabin as if she were expecting guests instead of preparing to leave the next day. She showered and then shampooed her hair, blow-drying it while clad in her red flannel nightie. Jade had just pulled back the blankets on the bed, when she looked up in surprise at the sound of an approaching car. It was followed by a knock on her front door.

"Jade? It's Steve."

"Steve," she said, answering his insistent pounding, "what's wrong?"

"I miss you, damn it," he yelled. "Why am I over there while you're over here?"

"Well, I—"

"And another thing! We live on the opposite ends of town in Detroit, and that stinks. I want to make love to you at night and wake up next to you in the morning! Are you listening to me?''

"Of course I am. Why are you yelling?"

"Because I feel like it!"

"That's a good reason, I guess," Jade mumbled.

"Therefore," Steve bellowed, causing Jade to cringe, "there is only one solution to this ridiculous situation."

"Oh?"

"Yes! I want you to marry me!"

"What!"

"You love me, right?"

"Yes, but—"

"And I love you, so that much is taken care of," Steve said, as he began to pace the floor. "I'm thirty-eight years old, Jade. I need a wife. You. I'd like a baby. Ours. I hate this slumber-party number we're doing with a night in your bed, another in mine. I'm sure as hell not going to work alongside you all day and then watch you drive off at five o'clock and then pick you up at seven for dinner. I'm not your damned date, I'm your lover, and I intend to be your husband!"

"Oh, is that so!" Jade said, planting her hands on her hips. "Do I have anything to say about this?"

"You're right, I'm going about this all wrong. Jade Emma Sinclair," Steve said softly, "will you marry me? Will you be my partner for life, forsaking all others until death parts us? I will cherish you, Jade, and I swear to God to never make you cry if I can help it. You have become my reason for being and I need you, want you, and love you more than there are words to say. Will you, Jade? Will you be my wife?"

Time stopped. The cabin faded into oblivion. Jade saw only one image. Steven Robert Chastain. She drew a shuddering breath and waited for her mind to begin its screaming turbulence, to shout at her to carefully analyze, to weigh and measure, Steve's words. But the clamor of voices remained silent and there was only a serene peace, a soothing warmth that settled over every fiber of Jade's being.

"Yes," she said, her voice a hushed whisper. "Yes, Steve, I'll marry you. I love you, and I will forever."

"Oh, Jade," he said, hugging her tightly against his hard chest. "We're going to be happy together. I promise you. We'll be married as soon as possible. Oh, unless you want one of those big fancy affairs with—"

"No, I hate those things. Just the two of us, Steve. It's a private special time."

"So are honeymoons," he said, grinning down at her.

"I've heard about those."

"We'll get away as quickly as we can, but I've already been gone from the business a long time."

"I understand. This time we spent in Dunrovin was our honeymoon. We just did things sort of in reverse."

"God, I love you."

"So! Which shall it be tonight? My place or yours, sport?"

"Since you're already in that god-awful nightgown, I guess I'll stay here."

"What's wrong with this nightie?"

"Emma would be proud of you, Jade." Steve chuckled. "You look very Victorian."

"Well! I'll have you know I'm going to have a dozen of these made up for when I become Mrs. Chastain."

"Go ahead. I'll enjoy every minute of taking them off."

"Starting when?"

"Now!" he said, scooping her up into his arms and heading for the bedroom. "Right now!"

Much later, the forgotten red flannel nightgown lay in a heap on the floor as Jade snuggled close to Steve, her hand resting on his chest so she could feel the steady beating of his heart. Their lovemaking had left them sated and sleepy and neither fought the drowsiness that crept over them.

"Steve?" Jade whispered.

"Hmmm?"

"What do you think of this idea?"

"Hmmm?"

"Buffy's Bagels!" Jade yelled, causing Steve to jerk straight up in bed.

"Good Lord!" he moaned, flopping back on the pillow. "I've created a monster! Good night, Jade!"

"Night, Steve," she said with a happy smile, and promptly fell asleep.

Eight

Jade ran her hand over the nape of her neck in an attempt to loosen her tired muscles and then gave up the effort as a lost cause. She reached for another file off the stack on her desk, opened it and stared at it with a gloomy expression on her face. She had been carefully studying every bit of information on the promotions that had been arranged for the athletes who were under contract with Steve's firm, with the hope of coming up with a fresh idea.

In the week since she and Steve had returned to Detroit from Dunrovin, she had accomplished nothing. Well, not exactly. She *had* become Mrs. Steve Chastain, and the brushed-gold wedding band on her left hand gave testimony to that fact. She was now totally moved into Steve's apartment and able to direct her attention at work to the subject at hand, Buffy Phillips.

Jade leaned back in her chair and tapped the eraser end of a pencil against her teeth, squinting as she stared at the ceiling. Somehow it seemed she was going at this all wrong. She was reviewing what all the other jocks— excuse me, gents—athletes had done instead of concentrating on what Buffy could do. To Jade he was nothing more than a few statistics on a sheet of paper. Maybe if she met the man, got an insight into his personality, she'd have a better concept of what would be appropriate for him to endorse.

"Steve?" Jade said into the intercom.

"Yes?"

"May I see you a minute?"

"Sure."

Jade stuck her tongue out at the intercom before walking briskly from the room. The very idea! Having to ask your own husband's permission to come into his office. Ridiculous!

"Hello, Mrs. Chastain," Steve greeted her. "Sit down and let me gawk at you."

"It's not in my contract." Jade laughed, her good mood instantly restored at the sight of Steve in his perfectly cut suit, his dark curls a raven glow on his head.

"How are you coming with Buffy Phillips?"

"Nada. Zip. Zero. Steve, I want to talk to Buffy, get to know him. I can't find a handle for this by reading files."

"I see," Steve said thoughtfully. "All right, set it up. He may be out of town because the Lions aren't due in training camp yet. I wanted definite proposals for him by the time he reported back."

"And if he's away?"

"Find him and we'll go to him."

"You'll come with me?"

"This first time? Yes, I won't throw you out on your own so soon. Okay?"

"Great. I'll start tracking him down."

"I made reservations for lunch. See you later."

"Right, boss," Jade said, saluting sharply.

"Hold it! I haven't done my sexual-harassment-on-the-job bit yet."

"But sir," Jade said, as Steve pulled her into his arms, "I'm a married woman."

"And don't you forget it," Steve said, kissing her deeply.

"Mr. Chastain, I . . . oh, excuse me," Suzanne said from the doorway.

"Yes, Suzanne?" Steve said, releasing a blushing Jade.

"I . . . I have these papers ready for your signature and . . . oh, I'm just so happy for you two. It's just like in one of my romance novels. I adore love stories and now I have one right here!"

"Thank you, Suzanne," Steve said, accepting the papers.

"Absolutely darling," Suzanne said, sniffling out the door.

"Well, what happened to her?" Steve said.

"Ain't love grand?" Jade said breezily, as she blew Steve a kiss and left the room.

There was no answer when Jade telephoned Buffy Phillips's home, so she called the office of the Detroit Lions football team. After explaining who she was and the importance of speaking with Buffy, Jade was informed that he was vacationing with his family in Stuart, Florida, and staying at The Groves Hotel.

"Ready for lunch?" Steve said some time later, poking his head in the door.

"I can't leave right now. I have a message in for Buffy at his hotel in Florida. I don't want to miss him."

"He'll find you later."

"That's not very professional, Steve. The least I can do is be here when he returns my call."

"You've got to eat."

"Could you bring me back a sandwich?"

"I suppose," he answered, frowning.

"Thanks."

Steve returned an hour later with a sandwich and a slice of pie for Jade, but before they could talk Suzanne summoned Steve for a long-distance call and a moment later told Jade that Buffy Phillips was on line three. With a tingle of excitement, Jade picked up the receiver and in her most businesslike voice told the football player she wished to meet him to discuss his contract. It was agreed that Jade would fly to Florida, and they scheduled a two o'clock appointment for the next day. Jade hung up with a satisfied nod of her head and reached for the intercom button to speak to Steve just as he came striding into the room.

"Pack your suitcase, my sweet," he said. "We're off to the wine country of Napa Valley, California."

"What?"

"That author I lined up to do the wine commercial came back from Europe early. It's now or never, because he's heading for Africa to research his next book. We fly out tonight."

"But we're going to Florida in the morning!"

"Damn," Steve said, raking his hair with his hand. "Well, postpone Phillips."

"Steve, no! I just set this up and it would be tacky to start shuffling him around. He's my client and I want to do this right."

"For God's sake, Jade, I want you with me! We'll be on opposite coasts of the country!"

"It's only for a few days, Steve. I don't like it any more than you do but it can't be helped."

Steve let out a long breath and shook his head, a deep frown on his face. "Yeah, okay," he said finally. "I guess we'll just have to go with it. This time. I'd better get home and pack."

"If my boss will give me the afternoon off, I'll come help you fold your shirts."

"I know how to fold shirts. What else can you do?"

"Oh, I'll think of something," she said, linking her arm through his. "Shall we go?"

There really was something to be said for being married to the boss, Jade thought dreamily, as she lay in the big bed watching Steve pack for his trip to California.

They had made sweet leisurely love upon arriving at the apartment, and then showered together, holding, kissing, caressing one another under the warm spray of water. Reluctantly, Steve had said he had to prepare to go, and Jade had climbed back into bed, where she lay with a lovely smile on her face.

"What happened to helping me pack?" Steve said, as he placed his clothes in the suitcase.

"I got a better offer."

"Lazy woman."

"Contented woman."

"You know, Jade, I'm not happy about our taking off in opposite directions like this. You're my wife first, my employee second."

"I intend to do the best I can in both roles, Steve."

"Just don't forget their order of importance."

"Quit scowling. Think about the beautiful reunion we'll have in a couple of days."

"I'll hang on to that thought."

"I'll get dressed and drive you to the airport," Jade said.

"No, I want to picture you lying there with your hair all tousled against the pillows and that lovely just-been-loved smile on your face. I'll take a taxi. You stay put."

"Now I do feel lazy."

"God, you are so beautiful," Steve said, sitting down on the edge of the bed. "I'll miss you, Jade. This separate-trip number isn't going to happen again."

"Good, because I'm getting lonely already."

"Oh, Jade," Steve said, pulling her close and kissing her with a fierce intensity that left her breathless. "That's it!" he yelled, getting up and grabbing his suitcase. "I'll chain you to my foot if I have to, but this is absolutely the last time we're being apart. Goodbye! I love you!"

"I love you, too!" Jade hollered after him, then flopped back onto the pillow with a wide silly smile on her face. Chain her to his foot! The heck with his foot, she'd rope herself to his entire body!

How had she functioned alone before Steve? Or was that how all of this worked? One minute you're a totally self-sufficient independent person. And then, when the time is right and that special person touches your heart, an unknown inner part of you emerges, needing and wanting to share, to laugh and cry with someone else. With Steve. And now, damn it, he was flying to one end of the country while she went in the other direction! Should she have postponed the meeting with Buffy Phillips and gone with Steve? No. She had been hired to do a job and she would do it. Not only that, she would execute it like a pro!

Jade slept restlessly that night, waking each time she reached for Steve in her sleep and her hand came to rest on the empty expanse of bed beside her. They had been married such a short time, but it was already unnatural, unsettling not to have his warm body within her grasp during the night. She finally rose before dawn, not willing to toss and turn another minute, and used the extra time to dust and straighten up the apartment. She knew the cleaning lady would be in the next day, but she needed an outlet for her nervous energy.

During the flight to Florida, Jade reviewed Buffy Phillips's biographical outline one more time, although she could practically recite it by heart. He was thirty-one years old and considering retirement after the upcoming season. He was six-foot-six, weighed two hundred and ninety-two pounds, was married and had a six-month-old daughter. The other information was a statistical breakdown of his impressive career in football, and under hobbies it said "Sports." That was it. A giant of a man with a narrow sphere of interests. There had to be something more to Buffy Phillips. Something unique that Jade could capitalize on and use to both their advantages.

Jade's suite at The Groves Hotel was pleasant and airy. She ate a quick lunch in the coffee shop before returning to her room to change into fresh clothes and wait for Buffy's arrival at two. She was excited about the forthcoming interview, and all earlier traces of nervousness had long since disappeared.

A knock on her door at exactly two o'clock brought her instantly to her feet, answering the summons with a smile. If the man standing before her was Buffy Phillips, he had shrunk to no more than five-foot-seven.

"Mrs. Chastain?"

"Yes."

"I'm the desk clerk. I just received a call from Mr. Phillips and he asked me to come up in person to deliver his message."

"Oh?"

"He drove up the coast with his family this morning and they developed car trouble. It will be tomorrow sometime before the repairs can be made and he can get back here. He's very sorry and hopes you understand."

"Yes, of course. Thank you." Wasn't that just hunky-dory, Jade thought as she shut the door. All dressed up and nowhere to go. Well, it was no one's fault, just one of those things.

Jade spent the remainder of the afternoon by the pool, and when she returned to her room the flashing light on her telephone indicated she had a message waiting at the front desk. The clerk informed her that Mr. Chastain had telephoned and wished her to return the call. Steve, however, was not at his hotel in California, and Jade had no choice but to repeat the dispatch in reverse. It was not turning out to be a terrific day.

Jade ate a quick dinner and hurried back to her room, hoping not to miss Steve's call. The evening stretched into slow-moving hours, and Jade finally gave up and went to bed at midnight after phoning Steve's hotel three times, only to learn he was not in. The shrill summons of the telephone woke her just before 2:00 A.M. and she groped for the receiver in the dark, mumbling a greeting.

"Jade?"

"Steve!" she said, instantly alert and snapping on the bedside lamp.

"We keep missing each other. How did it go?"

"Buffy had car trouble and I got postponed until tomorrow. And you?"

"Ditto. It's raining and the commercial is being done in a vineyard. Everything is on hold until the weather clears. I wined and dined our author to keep him happy."

"We both had lousy luck today."

"Come crawl in this bed, Jade. I want you next to me. Now. Right this minute."

"I wish I could. Believe me, I do. I love you, Steven Robert."

"I love you, too, Jade Emma, and I'm mad as hell that you're not here."

"I know," Jade said softly. "This bed is so big and lonely."

"You're killing me," Steve growled. "I'd better let you get some sleep. I'll call you tomorrow."

"Good night, Steve."

Jade replaced the receiver with a sigh and turned out the light, but sleep was now elusive as she ached for Steve, wanted him close, needed him to hold her in his arms. It was nearly dawn before she slept.

About the time Jade had decided that Buffy Phillips was a figment of her imagination, he showed up at her door just after noon. Boy, did he show up! The man was enormous, but much to Jade's surprise he was very soft-spoken and mild. He had a boyish grin and his first order of business was to whip out a dozen pictures of his baby daughter.

Jade enjoyed talking with the pleasant man, but was no further ahead in her assignment. The focus of Buffy's life was football and his family. Jade wanted to steer clear of the usual sports equipment endorsements that had been overdone by athletes, and Buffy was definitely not interested in a beer commercial because he never drank the stuff. He was basically a man who adored his wife and daughter and happened to play football as his chosen career. Nothing flashy. Nice, but rather dull from a selling standpoint. Unless . . .

"Buffy," Jade said suddenly, "I have an idea!"

By ten o'clock that night, Jade was a wreck. She was bubbling with excitement over her proposed plans for Buffy, but she couldn't reach Steve for his approval so she could set the wheels in motion. Damn, where was he? And why did she have to get his okay in the first place? Buffy was *her* client, *she* knew this was right for him, and she wanted to get started!

"Steve!" Jade said at 1:00 A.M. when he finally returned her call. "How are things there?"

"Wet."

"Oh, dear. Listen, I have it all figured out for Buffy."

"Oh?"

"Diapers."

"What?"

"Steve, the man is crazy about his baby. I've seen her and she's a doll. Buffy is a big gentle man whose life centers on his wife and daughter. Think about it! This hunk of a guy talking about wanting only the best for his kid and not being embarrassed to say he does his share of the diaper changing. We could use his own child in the commercial with him. Well?"

"Did you approach him about this?"

"Yes. He loves it."

"Sounds good, Jade."

"Great. I'll start contacting diaper companies tomorrow and see who's interested. You're still held up by the weather out there?"

"Yes, now we have fog just to make things interesting."

"Lovely. Well, I'll be home tomorrow night."

"I won't."

"You are definitely not in a good mood."

"Well, damn it, I miss you, Jade."

"And I miss you. Will you call me tomorrow?"

"Of course, but these little conversations aren't doing much for my libido."

"We'll make up for lost time, my dear Steven. I love you."

"Night, Jade."

Unable to get a flight to Detroit until four o'clock, Jade spent the next morning on the telephone talking to the advertising firms she was referred to by various diaper manufacturers. At noon she hit pay dirt. Darling Diapers was about to launch a campaign to promote their newest disposables, which were coming out in every color in the rainbow. Yes indeed, they would be interested in having Buffy Phillips endorse the product, and the addition of the football player's own daughter as a costar was perfect. All the Darling Diaper commercials were to be taped in St. Louis and, taking a deep breath, Jade agreed to be there in two days with the client and his baby in tow.

Jade was thrilled!

Steve was not.

"Thanks a lot," he roared when Jade called. "So now I go home to Detroit and find an empty apartment!"

"I had no choice! They're ready to start taping and—"

"You said yes!"

"Of course I did! This is perfect for Buffy."

"And me? What about me, Jade? Have you organized *us* into your schedule?"

"Damn it, Steve, that's a rotten thing to say. I'm only doing the job you assigned me to!"

"With your usual tunnel vision, seeing only the challenge at hand. Are you forgetting you're married now? Have a husband?"

"No! And I resent your implying such a thing. I've done a decent piece of work here. The contracts are being drawn up; the client is happy."

"Well, I'm not!"

"Steve, you're not being reasonable."

"Jade, I have to go. We'll discuss this at home when we're together. Which seems to be the major point in question here. Goodbye."

"Steve, wait! I... Damn," Jade said to the dial tone, and slammed the receiver into place. Steve was being ridiculous! How did he expect her to do a good job if he threw a fit because she did what was necessary? He was acting like a spoiled brat!

Jade was thoroughly depressed during the journey from Stuart to Detroit, and she was emotionally drained when she let herself into the empty apartment. She immediately called Steve's hotel in California and left a message for him when she was told he wasn't in. She was scheduled to fly to St. Louis the next morning, and Jade desperately wanted to talk to Steve before she left. No, more than that. She needed to see him, be swept into his strong embrace, and reach out to him during the night.

Jade stared at the telephone, willing it to ring, but it remained ominously silent, each hour ticking away with no word from Steve. She hardly slept, and the dark circles under her eyes the next morning gave testimony to that fact. Again she tried reaching Steve in California, only to be told by the desk clerk that Mr. Chastain was not in his room. Jade packed for the trip to St. Louis and, with one last look at the silent telephone, quietly left the apartment.

Three days later a thoroughly exhausted Jade reentered the living room and immediately pulled off her shoes. The taping of the diaper commercial had been . . . an experience. Buffy's daughter had taken one look at the bright lights and strange people and decided instantly that show business was not for her. The baby had wailed almost continually, causing constant delays in the proceedings. It wasn't until the morning of the third day that the infant had relaxed enough to play her role as a happy bundle in a Darling Diaper and the assignment had been completed.

Immediately upon arriving in St. Louis, Jade had telephoned Steve's hotel and left the number where she was staying. She waited that night for him to call, and when he did not, Jade made no further attempts to reach him.

Now, back in their home, Jade missed him with an intensity that was crushing, her heart aching as she walked through the empty apartment.

Everything had been so wonderful. She and Steve had glowed with happiness and Jade had found an inner peace she'd never dreamed possible. And then? God, what had happened? Jade had been over it a thousand times in her mind. Steve had hired her. He had personally decided she was to handle Buffy Phillips. And yet when Jade had proceeded to carry out her assignment to the best of her ability, Steve had become angry. He was even refusing to return her calls, had made no attempt to reach her in St. Louis.

Had Jade missed something? Why was Steve behaving so irrationally? She simply did not understand, and she wouldn't be able to until they had thoroughly discussed what had caused the horrible breach in their relationship. But how could she talk to him if he wasn't there? Surely it had stopped raining in Napa Valley by now. Why wasn't he home? Well, by damn, she wasn't calling California again to leave yet another message Mr. Chastain would ignore.

Jade was so exhausted she didn't have the energy to eat, so after a quick shower she crawled between the sheets. Maybe tomorrow she could sort it all out, make one more attempt to find Steve and ask him why he was behaving so strangely. But tonight there was no more emotional strength left. Not tonight.

When Jade awoke in the morning she realized she didn't know what to do. How could she go to the office and casually inform Suzanne that Steve was . . . sort of missing, that Jade had kind of mislaid her husband somewhere in California? Damn that Steven Robert. She'd like to punch him right in his gorgeous nose. Well, Jade decided, she was weary from her strenuous trip and deserved the day off. She'd stay home and relax. Relax? What a joke. She'd pace the floor, watch the clock and stare at the phone.

"Wonderful," Jade muttered, shuffling into the bathroom.

Later, dressed in jeans and a T-shirt, Jade settled on the sofa with a cup of coffee and toyed with the idea of painting her toenails. Forget it. Read a book? Watch a soap opera? Jump off the balcony? She had to do something, anything besides sit there brooding about Steve.

Suddenly the sound of a key turning in the lock brought her instantly to her feet and she stood, unable to move, as Steve entered the apartment and set his suitcase down inside the door. Jade couldn't speak; she simply stared at him, seeing the fatigue etched on his handsome face.

"Hello, Jade," he said quietly. "I see you made it home safely."

"Yes. I... Would you like a cup of coffee?"

"Yes, please."

"I'll get it," she said, hurrying to the kitchen. This was crazy! What was next? A little chitchat about the weather? The expression on Steve's face had told her nothing. It was blank. Tired and blank. And, yes, he'd like a cup of coffee. Sweet heaven, what was wrong with the man?

"Here you are," Jade said, handing the cup to Steve, who had slouched onto the sofa, his suit coat removed and his shirt half undone.

Oh, no you don't, Chastain, Jade thought fiercely. He wasn't going to start flashing that sexy body around. They had some serious talking to do.

"Did you wrap up the Phillips account?" Steve asked, not looking at her.

"Yes, it's all set. The commercials will start airing next month. Everyone involved was very pleased."

"And you?"

"I think it went well considering it was my first assignment."

"Of how many?" Steve asked, looking up at her where she stood several feet away.

"Pardon me?"

"Phillips will pass the word among the Lions, Jade, that you're good and get the job done. They'll start flocking to the company and asking to be handled personally by you. That's how it works. What happens then, Jade, when you're at the beck and call of a dozen football players, or their wives, or kids, or whoever they want you to represent?"

"Then, I suppose, I'll be doing what you hired me to do. My job is to promote people, isn't it, Steve? Or did I misinterpret what my role was in your company? Maybe you only took me on to decorate the place or add a wiggle to the scenery," Jade said, her voice rising.

"Damn it," Steve roared, getting to his feet, "you are my wife! First and foremost, you are Mrs. Steven Chastain! You should have been with me in Napa Valley, not holding some jock's hand in Florida and St. Louis. You belong with *me*!"

"Doing what? Smiling. Hanging on your arm and fluffing my so-called gorgeous hair? I don't understand you! I thought you'd be proud of what I accomplished for Buffy Phillips. You'd better spell this out for me, Steve, because I'm very confused. Do you, or do you not, want me to do the very best I can for the company?"

"No! No, damn it, I don't. It's happening, Jade. I can see it as clear as day. You're focusing in on that job and going at it nonstop. It's the old Jade Sinclair, organizing, analyzing, doing it up right with no sideways glances at anything or anyone else. Oh, you'll end up a top-notch promoter, right up there with the big boys. But along the way, Jade, you will have lost a husband!"

"What are you saying?" she whispered.

"I won't play second fiddle, have you only when you can fit me into your schedule."

"Then why did you hire me in the first place!"

"To have you near me. To give you something to do."

"Like a . . . a toy to play with to keep me out of trouble? The job was supposed to entertain me while you were busy, but my contribution wasn't really important and I was to drop everything when you whistled? Is that how you set it up, Steve?"

"I knew you wouldn't be happy sitting around here all day with nothing to do."

"So you pretended to create a position for me and let me believe you respected my intelligence and drive? God, what a joke. You must have gone into shock when I refused to change the itinerary I had made for Buffy Phillips. The game plan didn't include me doing a good job, did it? You assumed I'd drop everything and go off to Napa Valley with you."

"You're damn right I did. I thought you had changed, Jade. I really believed you'd seen the mistakes you had made with your unrelenting pursuit and wouldn't do it to yourself again. I thought *I* was the most important thing in your life now but I was wrong. No, Jade, I won't live this way. You're going to have to make a choice."

"Meaning?"

"Your *career* is this marriage. Your *job* is at the company. You take on one client at a time, and make it clear that he might be handled by someone else sometimes because you travel with your husband."

"My God, that's insulting!" Jade shrieked. "Little wifey gets to go to daddy's office if she's a good girl and has done the laundry and planned dinner before she leaves the house. But, oh, God forbid she does anything worthwhile at the big man's company. No, damn it, I won't do it! I won't pretend to work when what it would really amount to would be a farce. I'd be shuffling papers, waiting for you to snap your fingers and tell me what plane to get on.''

''I hired you, Jade, and I'm the one who can fire you!''

''Oh, no you can't, Steven Chastain, because... because I quit!''

''What!''

''You heard me!''

''Now wait just a damn minute here!''

''No! Your terms stink! I want to be your wife. That role is more important to me than I can begin to tell you. But I'm a person, too, a woman with intelligence and a need for an outlet for my capabilities. I won't be treated like a lamebrained piece of fluff who sits in a fancy office and counts paper clips. I function to my full potential or, by God, I don't function at all!''

''And just how do you plan to do that, Jade? When I met you, you had nowhere to go.''

''So you saved my poor, unfulfilled self by offering me a phony job? Well, thanks a million for your magnanimous gesture but you can keep it. I'm perfectly capable of taking care of myself!''

''Are you?'' Steve said, his voice suddenly deathly quiet. ''Are you really, Jade?''

An icy chill swept over Jade as she saw the tight set to Steve's jaw, the glint in his gray eyes that looked as hard as chips of flint. They stared at each other for a long tension-packed moment, then Steve turned, picked up his jacket and, without looking back, strode from the room and slammed the door roughly behind him.

Steve was gone. He had not touched, nor kissed, nor held Jade in his arms. He had announced in no uncertain terms that Jade's days of challenge, achievement and intellectual stimulation were over. She was a wife, and no more than that. What a fool she had been. For the first time in her life Jade had followed her heart instead of her mind and it was a disaster. She had tossed aside her natural instinct to carefully analyze, every detail of a situation and had simply closed her eyes and jumped in with both feet.

And now? She had nothing. Oh, not true, she thought bitterly. She had a broken heart. She had an undying love for a man she now realized she didn't really know. She had a lifetime sentence of loneliness that stretched before her like an insidious dark shadow.

Jade loved Steven with every fiber of her being, every breath in her body, but she could not live with him, stay at his side as an ornament, a decorative addition. She had believed he loved her as a total person, a lovely woman and an intelligent ambitious one. But it wasn't true. Like the parade of escorts who had seen only her surface beauty, so had Steve. He had ignored all the inner feelings Jade had shared with him, her needs and wants, the giving of her very soul. He saw now only the golden hair, the lush figure, the enchanting smile. He wanted her body. Her mind be damned.

Jade didn't move, or cry, or hardly breathe. She just stood there as if she had stepped outside of herself and was watching her world crumble. She had loved. God, how she had loved him, would always love him. And she had lost. The pain was numbing, immobilizing, beyond description in its intensity.

She pressed her fingertips to her aching temples and tried desperately to sort through the jumbled maze in her mind. She had to think. She had to! How had this happened? Where had it all gone wrong? She needed some time alone to seek the answers to the questions that hammered at her. She wouldn't find them there in Steve's apartment, with memories of Steve confronting her at every turn.

As if in slow motion, Jade picked up the coffee cups and walked into the kitchen, where she washed them and placed them carefully in their proper place in the cupboard. She moved slowly through the apartment, straightening a chair, fluffing a pillow, putting everything in order.

In the bedroom she changed into a simple dark dress and coiled her hair into a tight chignon at the nape of her neck. Giving in to a single shuddering sob, she pulled the gold wedding band from her finger and set it on the dresser with a trembling hand.

And then slowly, methodically, she took her suitcase from the closet and began to pack.

Nine

Jade sipped a glass of lemonade as she glanced around the living room of Granny's cabin and nodded her head in approval. Everything was fresh and clean and the musty odor from having been closed up and neglected had dissipated. Jade had arrived late the night before and for the first time in a month had slept soundly, awakening at dawn to restore order to the cabin.

One month. Four long weeks since that heart-wrenching scene with Steve in their apartment in Detroit. After closing the door on her life as Mrs. Steve Chastain, Jade had spent the ensuing days in a hotel seeing and speaking to no one except her attorney. He had been shocked when he received Jade's telephone call, and had tried to convince Jade to change her mind. But she had stood firm in her resolve. She was selling all three of the Grandmother's Cottage boutiques.

Jade had felt an inner calm when she put her signature on the contracts of sale. Beth and the others had been guaranteed their positions and the new owners had a genuine interest in maintaining the high quality of the stores.

"But why, Jade?" her lawyer had asked. "Granted, you made a fabulous profit, but—"

"It's time," Jade had said quietly, and would offer no further explanation.

But Jade knew the reason that the boutiques no longer had a place in her life. To her they represented tangible visible evidence of the error of her ways. Her single-mindedness, her drive and obsession to succeed, had created the three lucrative shops but had also helped form the woman Jade no longer wished to be. The boutiques had grown from a seed of thought in her mind, been born, nurtured until they thrived, and left Jade empty and alone with no purpose or direction to her life.

Jade's abilities had been channeled in a straight line. She had seen only the goal at the end and had not rested until it had been achieved. It had brought her financial reward and an empty soul. And then, at the most vulnerable time in her life, she had met Steve. Steven Robert Chastain with his rugged good looks and curly hair, his ready smile and throaty chuckle, and Jade had fallen in love forever.

But ambition had reared its head once again and snared Jade in its miscreant clutches. She had been determined to become a first-rate promoter, to excel in her new field, place her challenge above everything else, forsaking all others. Forsaking her Steve. He had seen the signs, the nefarious enemy staking its claim on his wife, and demanded she return to his side to share in his life, be his partner, and Jade had refused. She would succeed at her profession and no one would stand in her way. And so Steve had left her so she could live with her accomplishments instead of with him.

If only Steve hadn't stormed out of the apartment when he was so angry. Their tempers had flared, and then he had left her before they could quietly examine what had happened. He'd had his say, screamed his biting words, then stalked off like a child in the middle of a tantrum. They both had made mistakes, and they were paying a tremendous price for their actions.

And now Jade was alone. Older, wiser, but alone. During the month in the quiet hotel, she had cried until there were no more tears. She had raged in anger, sobbed in desolation, screamed in her solitude, and then stopped. In a slow process of healing and self-examination she had mentally retraced her life, seen her mistakes in crystal clarity, and planned her future with a firm new resolve.

Never again would she close herself off from the beauty and gifts of the world around her as she set about her daily life. She would encompass it all, be whole, capable of giving and taking in equal portions. The lessons had been learned, but the understanding had come too late. She had lost the only man she had ever loved.

Jade ached for Steve, saw his image nightly in her dreams, reaching for him and suffered through the tears because he was no longer there. She had relived that final scene in their apartment a thousand times in her mind, hearing Steve tell her he needed, wanted her as his wife.

God, how clear it all was. What she had then viewed as selfishness and condescension on Steve's part, Jade now saw as a man desperately fighting for a place in his woman's existence. He wanted a wife, not a corporate executive, and had literally pleaded with her to stay by his side, travel with him, share his bed at night and wake up next to him in the morning. But Jade had refused.

Over the past weeks, Jade had created scenarios in her mind in which she'd stroll into Steve's office and calmly announce she had come to terms with their problems. Steve would leap over the top of his desk, pull Jade into his arms, and declare his undying love. It was a fantasy all right. Jade had dealt a lethal blow to Steve's pride and ego. Her actions had told him that he took a back seat to her ambitions. Steve would never believe that she had changed, would never again trust her. And so it was over.

"Oh, Granny," Jade whispered, staring at the empty rocker, "I love Steve so much. He laughed in this cabin, Granny, and we loved so dearly here. You would have liked my Steve."

Angrily brushing a tear from her cheek, Jade left the cabin and headed for Ben McKenna's store for groceries. Jade knew Ben would ask where Steve was, and she was sure she would never get through her explanation without sobbing, but she had to face Ben sometime. She only hoped that Mrs. Steinberg had decided to take a trip to the moon.

"Hello, Ben," Jade said quietly when she entered the store, immediately grateful that there was no one else there.

"Jade!" Ben said, coming from behind the counter and hugging her. "I'd about given you up for dead! Lord, child, you had us worried sick."

"Why?"

"Steve has called me every day, every single day for the past month, asking if you had showed up in Dunrovin."

"Steve...has been looking for me?" Jade asked, her voice hushed.

"The man is frantic. Sit down, Jade. I'll get you a root beer and then you talk to your old Ben. It appears you've gotten yourself in a fine kettle of fish this time."

"You could say that." Jade nodded miserably, sinking onto one of the rockers.

Jade cried, got the hiccups, and cried some more as she related her tale of woe to Ben, who listened with a scowl on his wrinkled face.

"Yep, you did it up good," he said, when she finally sniffled her story to a close. "Well, fix it!"

"I can't, Ben. It's too late. Steve would never believe me now. He'd be watching me every minute for signs that my role as his wife was beginning to bore me. There would always be that tension between us. He'd examine everything I did. He'd be a warden, not a husband. It's over, Ben. I made terrible mistakes that I can't undo. I have a new plan for my life. I'll rest here for a bit and then move on."

"Alone?"

"I have no choice."

"Steve has phoned every day—or didn't that get through that stubborn head of yours?"

"I...can't imagine why he did that. He's hurt and angry. He certainly doesn't want to see me again."

"I love the way you decide what the man is thinking. Why would he be calling? To tell you to pick up your cleaning? Oh, I wish Granny was here to whack sense into you! You are acting like a fool."

"You don't understand, Ben."

"Oh, is that right? I've got news for you, Jade Emma, you are not so all-fired smart. I've done a few more years of livin' in this world than you have, and I'm telling you to go to that Steve and talk to him!"

"So he can tell me to get lost? No thanks," Jade said, getting up and walking to the door. "Throw a bunch of food in a box and have Billy Haskins deliver it, okay?"

"I suppose," Ben grumbled.

"Thanks for the root beer."

"Thanks for the headache. Jade, you're more trouble to me than if you were my own kid."

Jade walked back to the cabin with her hands shoved into the pockets of her jeans. Steve had been calling every day? Why? Could he have been worried about her? Thought she'd jumped into the Detroit River? Lord, was he trying to find her to give her their divorce papers? Divorce. What an ugly word. But it was inevitable. They had no marriage and Steve was probably anxious to be a free agent again. Busybody Ben would tell Steve that Jade had at least arrived in Dunrovin, that was for sure. Then what? Steve's lawyer shows up and says, "Sign here and let's get this farce over with"? Damn it, she didn't want a divorce. She wanted to be Steve's wife and have his baby. And she could have done it all with the new plans she had formulated. Wife, mother, everything. But it was too late.

Back at the cabin, Jade wandered into the second bedroom and stood staring at the trunk that held Emma's letters to Charles. The memories of the time spent with Steve working on the intriguing project assaulted her, and she lifted the lid with a trembling hand. She had promised not to read any of the letters unless Steve was there to share in the discoveries, but those days were behind her. Emma, Charles and Henry belonged only to Jade again. She carried the stack of plastic folders into the living room, settled herself on the sofa and began to read.

It was after midnight when Jade carefully placed the last letter on the stack and drew a shaking breath. She had stopped only long enough to put away the groceries Ben had sent with Billy Haskins and then returned immediately to the sofa, giving no thought to eating dinner.

Emma's life had unfolded before Jade's eyes and Jade had been mesmerized by the words on the yellowed sheets. Emma had mapped out a detailed plan for hers and Charles's life together. They would homestead in northern Michigan, raise a family and live happily ever after. Charles was to farm the land, provide for his wife and children, and that was the way it was going to be. Emma even described the cabin Charles would build and rattled on about how the furniture would be arranged. Emma was organized.

But Charles had dreams of his own and had set out for the gold country of California to make his fortune, asking Emma to wait until he returned. In each letter Emma became more hostile, more demanding. She had everything figured out and, by God, Charles had best forget his foolishness and get himself home. Emma could see only her goal, gave no thought to Charles's needs or wants. And then in the final letter Emma had stated she would wait no more. She had met a man named Henry who was willing to comply with all of Emma's wishes, and she was going to marry him. Charles had not played by her rules so he couldn't have her. It was Emma's way or not at all and Charles was removed from the scene.

"My God," Jade whispered in the quiet room, "I was Emma. I did to Steve what she did to Charles. And we lost our loves, Emma. We lost."

Whether Emma had ever regretted her decision to marry Henry, Jade could not know. Perhaps Granny's mother had never changed, had directed Henry's life until the day she died. But Jade *had* changed. She recognized her mistakes and grieved for the man who would never again smile down at her, hold her in his powerful arms or make exquisite love to her.

Jade walked wearily into the bedroom and threw herself across the bed, not bothering to remove her clothes. She fell asleep instantly and, as she had every night for the past month, dreamt of Steve. The next morning she showered, dressed in jeans and a cotton shirt and brushed her hair until it was a shining cascade down her back. After replacing Emma's letters in the trunk, she set off for a walk in the woods.

It was time to leave Dunrovin. It was time to put into action her new plans. And it was time to place in a special space in her mind the mistakes both she and Emma had made so they would never be repeated. Jade would move forward, learn to smile again, and pray that someday the ache in her heart for Steven Robert Chastain would diminish.

Her wanderings brought her back onto the dirt road leading to her cabin, and she suddenly realized she was at the spot where she had found Steve when he was a "dead" body. On impulse, she pushed through the bushes and sank to her knees onto the soft grass, the image of Steve dancing before her eyes. As a sob caught in her throat, she stretched out on her back and watched the sun through the fluttering leaves of the tree. The tree. This place where Steve had declared her to be a pickpocket and then kissed her until she was unable to think straight. So many memories of loving times. So many. Jade's eyelids grew heavy, and to the serenade of chirping birds, she slept.

"Jade?" It was Steve's voice, and it accompanied the vision of him in Jade's dream. "Jade, please wake up." To wake was to lose the picture of her Steve that was in her mind, and she didn't want to let it go. But something was wrong. A hand was gripping her arm, and that wasn't happening in the dream. "Jade!"

"What?" she yelled, sitting bolt upright, her face only inches away from Steve Chastain's, who was kneeling beside her. "Steve? Steve?"

"Hello, Jade," he said quietly, turning around and sitting with his back against the trunk of the tree. "I'm sorry if I startled you. When you weren't at the cabin I decided to come visit this spot while I was waiting for you. I didn't expect you to be here."

"Ben told you I was in Dunrovin," Jade said, her eyes sweeping over Steve's magnificent form in faded jeans and a blue shirt that lent its color to his eyes. Her glance caught the fatigue etched on his handsome face and she frowned slightly. Then she saw the large brown envelope lying on the grass, and a wave of icy misery swept over her. He had brought the divorce papers himself instead of sending his lawyer. In a few fleeting minutes she would no longer be Mrs. Steve Chastain.

"I've been trying to find you for a month, Jade," Steve said, his voice hushed.

"Yes, Ben told me," Jade said, tearing her gaze from the envelope. "I'm sorry if I inconvenienced you."

"Inconvenienced! Jade, I was sick with worry! I had no idea where you were. It's been a nightmare. I've got to talk to you, Jade."

"Just give me the papers, Steve. I won't ask anything of you in the way of support."

"What papers?"

"In that envelope. That's why you came, isn't it? To have me sign divorce forms?"

"Is that what you want?" he asked, a muscle twitching in his jaw.

"No! I mean, I . . ."

"Jade, I love you. I will always love you. Come back to me, babe, please. My life has been so empty since you left. God, I made such terrible mistakes. I tried to change you into something you couldn't be and then became angry when you didn't conform. Jade, I don't care if you work for me or run ten businesses of your own. I understand now that you have to have a challenge, an outlet for your intelligence and drive. We'll make whatever time is left over for us very special and—"

"Steve, no!"

"I won't try to hold you back, I promise! Give me another chance."

"Steve, you're not understanding," Jade said, brushing sudden tears off her cheeks. "I need to be with you. I want to be your wife and have your baby."

"Oh, Jade, don't try to be something you can't be. You'll grow restless and bored and start looking for more. Let's be honest about this and face the facts as they are. I'll learn to be satisfied with whatever moments we share."

"Steve, please listen to me! So much has happened since that awful argument we had. I . . . sold all three of the Grandmother's Cottages."

"Why? You built them up from scratch."

"They nearly destroyed me, like everything else I set out to do. I've had time to think and examine my life. Not only mine, but Emma's too."

"Emma's? You read the letters?"

"Yes, and she was so wrong. She organized her and Charles's existence down to the last detail, and when he didn't comply with her wishes she tossed him away and married Henry. I'd like to think she was happy with him, but I honestly don't feel she was. I made the same mistakes Emma did, but maybe... it's not too late for me."

"What are you saying, Jade?"

"Steve, I have a gift! I can size up a situation, analyze it, determine its needs and see it through to its end. Don't you see? I never again have to be empty and restless because I've overachieved myself right out of being useful."

"I don't understand."

"Steve, I'm going to teach! I'm opening a school for management skills. I'll never be finished, Steve, because there will always be people who will want to learn. Each new student will be a challenge and it will go on and on. I'll hire the finest teachers for my staff and I'll be free to travel with you whenever you go. Except, of course, when I'm very pregnant and can't get on an airplane. Oh, Steve, don't you see? I can have my challenges and still be a real wife for you."

In a motion so quick it caused Jade to gasp in surprise, Steve reached out his long arms and hauled her across the grass and onto his lap. His mouth claimed hers in a kiss that was fierce in its intensity, a kiss that spoke of the pain and loneliness and empty hours he had endured. And then it gentled into a soft sensuous embrace that brought a moan from Jade's throat as she leaned into the hard contours of his body.

"Oh, Jade," he murmured. "My Jade. I do love you so much."

"I am so sorry, Steve, for what I did to us. If only I had read Emma's letters years ago. Forgive me, please."

"And I'm asking for your forgiveness. I handled things so badly. I thought I had lost you forever."

"I hope our babies all have dark curls."

"Only the boys. The girls have to have wheat-colored hair like their mother."

"Steve, those papers in the envelope, are they...?"

"No, Jade," he said, setting her back up on the grass. "Randy sent me the pictures he took of you that day on the beach. One was so special I had it enlarged. Open it."

Jade pulled out the photograph and stared at it for several minutes. The wind had whipped her hair into a golden halo and she was smiling, a serene lovely smile that matched the warm expression in her eyes. One hand was slightly lifted as if reaching out to receive something precious into her grasp. The picture spoke one word—love.

"It's all there," she whispered. "What I feel for you, how much I love, and need, and want you."

"I brought it to show you, Jade, with the hope you'd remember how it had been. We were so happy, and I so desperately wanted another chance to bring this beautiful expression to your face. It's there now, I can see it. Say it, Jade. Say you'll never leave me again."

"Oh, I won't! I love you, Steven Robert Chastain, and I will forever."

"There's something else in that envelope."

Jade reached down into the corner and with trembling fingers withdrew her wedding band. Steve took it from her and lifted her hand.

"With this ring I pledge my love until there is no breath left in my body," he said huskily, tears glistening in the blue pools of his eyes. "Will you be my wife?"

"I will," Jade whispered, tears clinging to her lashes, while Steve slipped the ring onto her finger.

"I want to make love to you, Jade, here in this place where I met you for the first time."

"But you were a 'dead' body!"

"Believe me, I am very much alive."

"Prove it."

Steve Chastain was certainly alive and well. He came to Jade with a power that consumed her instantly, sent her desire soaring to a fever pitch, and brought the sound of his name from her lips. As they soared higher, away from reality, they left behind the hurt and confusion that had plagued them, never to be felt again. They rediscovered and claimed as their own the mysteries of each other, relished the feel and aroma of the one most important to their world. Afterward they lay close, hands resting possessively on one another, neither wishing to break the aura of contentment that shrouded them.

"I suppose," Steve said finally, "we should think about heading back."

"It's so lovely here."

"It will always be our special place. Let's go see Ben. I've hounded him to death for the past month about you. He deserves to know our happy ending."

"I'll come on one condition," Jade said.

"Which is?"

"You buy me a root beer!"

"I'll buy you a lifetime of root beers, Jade Emma. You know, it's so appropriate that we met in this little town by the lake. I had been searching for you all of my life and now I truly am... Dunrovin."

"I love you, Steven Robert," Jade whispered. "I love you."

 # Silhouette Desire

COMING NEXT MONTH

THE FIRE OF SPRING—Elizabeth Lowell
Winning the Sheridan ranch wasn't enough for vengeful
Logan Garrett—he wanted Dawn Sheridan, too. Dawn was
determined to teach him to love, not hate, and she'd accept
nothing less.

THE SANDCASTLE MAN—Nicole Monet
Sharon wanted a child—Michael's child, but Michael was gone.
Then one day Sharon met Rob Barnes, who became her fairy-tale
prince . . . but would reality intrude on their dreams?

LOGICAL CHOICE—Amanda Lee
Analytically minded Blake Hamilton was surprised when he
discovered his attraction to Diana Adams couldn't be explained
away. Diana had to show him just how illogical love could be!

CONFESS TO APOLLO—Suzanne Carey
Denying her own Greek heritage, Zoe planned to quickly leave
her childhood home after a business trip there. Then she met
Alex Kalandris—devastatingly handsome, utterly compelling
and—Greek.

SPLIT IMAGES—Naomi Horton
After TV spokeswoman Cassidy York interviewed arrogant
Logan Wilde and got blackmailed, on-air, into a date with him,
she was enraged. But meeting the man behind the image
engendered very different emotions.

UNFINISHED RHAPSODY—Gina Caimi
When concert pianist Lauren Welles returned home to her former
music teacher, Jason Caldwell, she realized she still had a lot
more to learn. . . . But not about music.

AVAILABLE NOW:

OUT OF THIS WORLD
Janet Joyce

DESPERADO
Doreen Owens Malek

PICTURE OF LOVE
Robin Elliott

SONGBIRD
Syrie A. Astrahan

BODY AND SOUL
Jennifer Greene

IN THE PALM OF HER HAND
Dixie Browning